CASCADING DIVERGENCE
1941 Lebensraum

THE ALTERNATE HISTORY CONTINUES
INVASION OF THE SOVIET UNION

by
RON WOOD

RON WOOD

CASCADING DIVERGENCE 1941 Lebensraum

Copyright © 2025 by Ron Wood

All rights reserved.

No portion of this book may be reproduced in any form without written permission from the author, except as permitted by U.S. copyright law.

ISBN:

979-8-89901-150-4 (ebook)

979-8-89901-151-1 (paperback)

979-8-89901-154-2 (hardcover)

First Edition: April 2025

CASCADING DIVERGENCE 1941 Lebensraum

Dedicated to my grandchildren.

May you always know peace and never endure the shadows of war. Face life with logic, seek truth with reason, and question with curiosity. In a world often swayed by passion and impulse, let critical thinking be your guide, wisdom your strength, and knowledge your shield.

RON WOOD

TABLE OF CONTENTS

PROLOGUE: Looking Eastward 1
1 Grand Deception 7
2 A Sleeping Bear 15
3 The Ruse..27
4 Stalin's Growing Overconfidence 43
5 The Calm Before the Storm 53
6 The First Blows 65
7 Red Army in Chaos...73
8 Soviet Counterattack...87
9 Road to Smolensk 99
10 Fall of Smolensk..109
11 Drive to Moscow 121
12 Siege of the Capital 131
13 Moscow Falls...143
14 Aftermath of the Fall...153
EPILOGUE: Expanding Divergence..................................167
The Alternate History Continues...171
About the Author...172
Acknowledgments..174

RON WOOD

Invasion Plan–1941

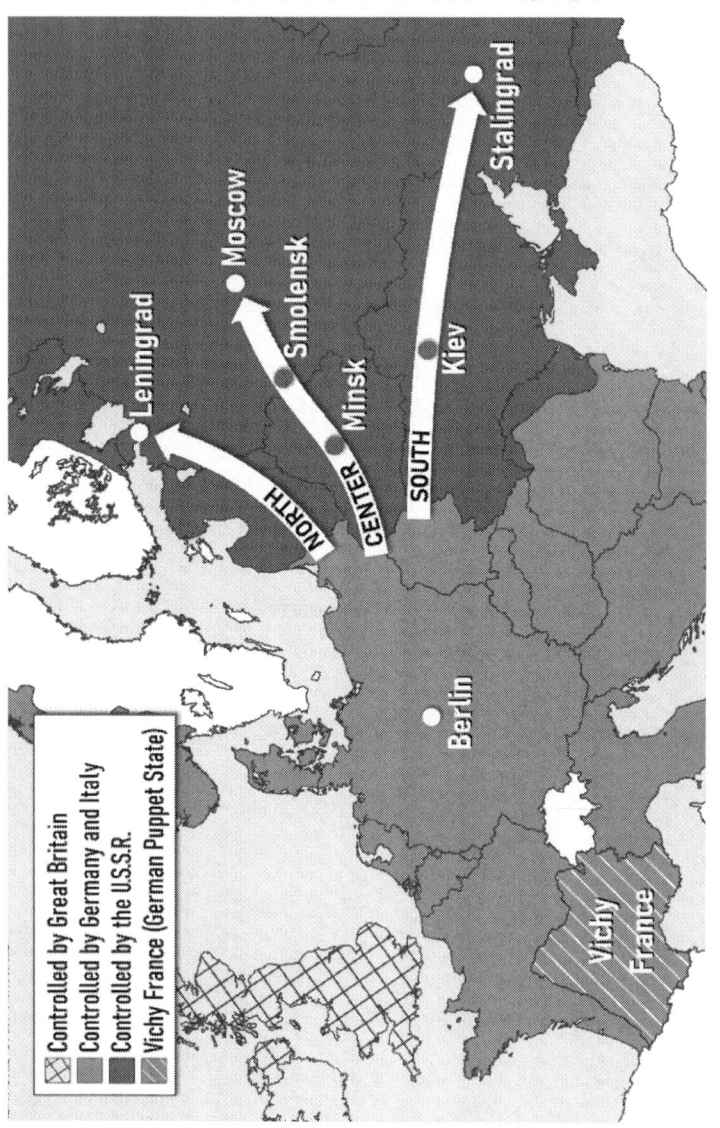

PROLOGUE:
Looking Eastward
December 1940, Berlin

I. As It Really Happened

For Hitler, war in the East wasn't just inevitable—it was destiny. He didn't see the Soviet Union as merely an adversary; he saw it as the final obstacle standing between Germany and its rightful place as a continental empire. In his vision, the Reich would stretch from the Atlantic to the Urals, and for that to happen, Russia had to be erased.

But this wasn't just about land. It was about ideology, race, and resources. To Hitler, Bolshevism wasn't just a political system—it was a disease that needed eradication. The Slavs? A people to be subjugated. The vast Soviet lands? Germany's future breadbasket and fuel depot. This wasn't a conventional war; it was a crusade to reshape the world.

From this vision came Operation Barbarossa—the largest military invasion in history. The goal? Total annihilation of the Soviet Union in mere months. No drawn-out war, no slow attrition—just a swift, decisive blow that would leave Stalin's empire in ruins. After all, hadn't France collapsed in just six weeks? Why should the Soviet Union be any different?

The Plan for Conquest

Barbarossa was a behemoth of an operation, involving over three million Axis soldiers, thousands of tanks, and the full might of the Luftwaffe. It was split into three prongs, each with a critical mission:

- **Army Group North** (commanded by Field Marshal von Leeb): Capture Leningrad and cut the Soviets off from the Baltic.
- **Army Group Center** (led by Field Marshal Fedor von Bock): Take Moscow—the heart of the Soviet Union. The belief was that if Moscow fell, the entire Soviet system would unravel.
- **Army Group South** (under Field Marshal Gerd von Rundstedt): Seize Ukraine, with its vast farmland and crucial oil fields. Starving Soviet industry and cutting off their war machine was as important as battlefield victories.

The key was speed. Blitzkrieg—lightning war—had shattered Poland and France. The same formula would break the Soviet Union before they had time to react.

German intelligence assured Hitler of an easy victory. Stalin had purged his own officer corps, leaving the Red Army in disarray. Their weapons? Outdated. Their tactics? Clumsy. Hitler was so convinced of success that he boasted the entire campaign would be over in weeks.

A War of Miscalculations

But it wasn't. Barbarossa failed.

The first mistake? Delay. The invasion was originally set for May 1941, but Hitler's attention drifted. Instead of focusing on the East, he had to clean up Mussolini's failures in the Balkans. By the time Barbarossa finally launched on June 22, 1941, the Soviets had gained precious time.

CASCADING DIVERGENCE 1941 Lebensraum

At first, it seemed like the Germans had been right. The Red Army crumbled in battle after battle. Entire Soviet divisions were encircled and destroyed. Three million Soviet soldiers were captured within months. German tanks pushed deep into Soviet territory, advancing hundreds of miles at breakneck speed.

And yet—the Soviet Union didn't collapse.

Instead, it did something the Germans hadn't anticipated: It endured.

Germany had catastrophically underestimated the scale of the war.

The vast distances overstretched supply lines.

Soviet scorched-earth tactics denied the Germans resources.

Soviet rail systems ran on a different gauge, slowing down logistics.

Poor infrastructure bogged down German movement in ways Blitzkrieg wasn't designed for.

Then Hitler made it worse. Instead of pressing on to Moscow, he became obsessed with Ukraine's resources, diverting vital forces south. This slowed the momentum just as Soviet resistance stiffened.

By autumn, the skies darkened, and the *rasputitsa*—the infamous Russian mud—began. Roads turned to sludge, and the Germans—so reliant on mechanized movement—ground to a halt.

Then came winter.

Temperatures plummeted to -40°C (-40°F).

Engines seized as fuel froze.

Weapons jammed.

German soldiers, unprepared for Arctic conditions, froze to death in their summer uniforms.

Meanwhile, the Soviets adapted. Siberian reinforcements—hardened by extreme cold—arrived. Stalin's armies counterattacked. The Germans, exhausted and under-equipped, were pushed back from the gates of Moscow.

By December 1941, it was clear: Barbarossa had failed. The quick, crushing victory Hitler had envisioned was gone. Instead of conquest, Germany found itself trapped in a war it wasn't prepared to fight—a war of attrition on a scale never before seen.

In our history, this was the beginning of the end for the Third Reich. The Soviets only grew stronger, and by 1945, it was the Red Army that marched into Berlin.

II. The Divergent Timeline–as of 1940 Year's End

But here, this timeline is different.

History won't unfold the way we remember.

As detailed in the first story of the saga (*Cascading Divergence 1940 An Alternate World History Begins*), by the end of 1940, the war in Europe had taken a dramatic and unexpected turn. Following the sudden death of Winston Churchill in a

CASCADING DIVERGENCE 1941 Lebensraum

German bombing raid, Britain's government, deeply divided and without its most resolute leader, chose to negotiate.

In December, the Treaty of Geneva was signed between Britain and Germany, formally ending hostilities between the two powers. The British Empire remained intact, while Germany secured dominance over continental Europe without the need for further conflict in the West.

With Britain neutralized, Adolf Hitler turned his full attention eastward. He called it *Lebensraum*—"living space"—the land that would fuel Germany's expansion and secure its future as a world power.

With no Western Front to hold him back, Hitler could focus on his plan for Operation Barbarossa, the largest and most ambitious invasion in history.

RON WOOD

1

Grand Deception
January–February 1941 – Berlin, Germany

In the streets outside the Reich Chancellery, the night was still. A bitter wind swept down Wilhelmstraße, laced with the scent of iron and coal from Berlin's factories. The great stone structure loomed above, guarded by SS men whose boots barely disturbed the frost-laced pavement.

Inside, deep within a fortress of marble and steel, Germany's most powerful men were gathering.

The Grand Conference Room was shrouded in heavy silence. A chandelier threw dim light over the polished surface of a vast mahogany table. Around it, the architects of war took their seats. The oaken doors were bolted behind them.

Adolf Hitler sat at the head, rigid and brooding. His fingers were interlaced on the table. He did not speak. He watched.

To his right lounged Reichsmarschall Hermann Göring, Supreme Commander of the Luftwaffe. Once lean and heroic, Göring had grown bloated on privilege. His ornate uniform shimmered with medals, his jowls trembled with each lazy grin. Outwardly amused by the proceedings, inwardly he brooded over the Luftwaffe's failure in the Battle of Britain. He welcomed the Eastern campaign as a chance for redemption, a fresh arena where air power might redeem his legacy—and silence his detractors.

Across from Göring sat Joachim von Ribbentrop, Reich Minister for Foreign Affairs. A man of elegant suits and empty eyes, Ribbentrop spoke in the calm tones of diplomacy but calculated always in terms of leverage. He had spent two years preserving Germany's pact with Stalin, though he now saw that partnership as nothing more than a delaying tactic. He believed the Soviets could be outplayed, and he had fed Stalin just enough misinformation to let him walk blindfolded into the trap.

Farther down the table, Heinrich Himmler, Reichsführer of the SS and Chief of German Police, sat motionless, fingers steepled. His skin was papery, his stare unsettlingly blank. He viewed the Eastern war not merely as conquest, but as purification—an ideological cleansing that would give rise to a racial empire. In his mind, the Waffen-SS would soon outshine the Wehrmacht. Every city razed, every village repopulated, would bring that vision closer.

At Hitler's left sat Field Marshal Wilhelm Keitel, Chief of the High Command of the Armed Forces (OKW). Impeccably uniformed, posture perfect, Keitel was the image of obedience. He spoke only when called upon, and then only to affirm. He neither questioned nor advised. His loyalty was absolute, but it masked a shallow, strategic mind. He would sign anything, and had.

Beside him sat General Alfred Jodl, Chief of Operations Staff at the OKW. He flipped through a thick folder of briefing papers, brows furrowed, lips pursed. Jodl was an

CASCADING DIVERGENCE 1941 Lebensraum

analytical mind caught in a political machine. He had orchestrated operations across Europe with clinical precision, but inside he harbored growing unease. He doubted Hitler's instinctual style of warfare, doubted the sheer scale of what was being proposed—but he buried those doubts beneath protocol and performance.

Around the far side of the table sat the generals.

Field Marshal Fedor von Bock, commander of Army Group Center, was gaunt, grim, and utterly professional. He wore his decorations without vanity. Politics bored him; ideology repelled him. He saw war as craft and execution. His mind was already marching toward Moscow, which he believed was the true heart of Soviet resistance. If it fell quickly, the entire state might collapse.

Next to him was Field Marshal Gerd von Rundstedt, commander of Army Group South. The oldest of the senior commanders, Rundstedt exuded quiet caution. He had fought in the Great War and seen the cost of overreach. Though respectful in tone, he had little faith in Hitler's intuition and often viewed Himmler's ideological bluster with veiled disdain. In his estimation, Ukraine was the key— its wheat, coal, and oil would feed the Reich and starve the Soviets.

Beside him, Field Marshal Wilhelm von Leeb, commander of Army Group North, sat with arms crossed, lips drawn tight. A devout Catholic and the second-eldest officer present, Leeb was increasingly disturbed by the moral decay creeping into the upper echelons of command. He viewed the war in the East with trepidation, not out of fear, but because he sensed it would stain everything it touched. Still, duty was duty.

The room pulsed with silence.

Hitler leaned forward at last.

"The time has come," he said, voice low but sharp. "The war against Bolshevism is inevitable. We must strike first—and finish it."

A rustle of movement.

Keitel cleared his throat. "Mein Führer, planning is underway. But what of Stalin? Is he aware? Will we continue our deception?"

Hitler nodded slowly, a cruel flicker in his eye. "Not just with deception, Keitel. With certainty. Stalin will see exactly what we want him to see."

He gestured to Ribbentrop.

"The diplomatic channels remain intact," Ribbentrop reported. "Stalin still believes we are allies. Trade continues. Oil, grain, metals. Soviet leadership senses no threat."

"And the border?" Hitler asked.

Jodl unfurled a map across the table. Inked lines marked German troop deployments and Soviet observation points.

"We're constructing fortifications—trenches, minefields, bunkers. All visible. Soviet reconnaissance will report defensive buildup, not preparation for attack."

Göring chuckled dryly. "Let them think we're cowering."

CASCADING DIVERGENCE 1941 Lebensraum

Ribbentrop continued. "We've let Soviet spies observe industrial bottlenecks—some real, most fabricated. Stalin believes we are overextended. The NKVD dismisses warnings of invasion as disinformation."

Hitler's smile was thin and cold. "And the Wehrmacht?"

Keitel nodded. "Troop deployments are on schedule. Over three million men by spring. Army Group North in East Prussia. Center in Poland. South in Romania."

The table fell still.

Then Hitler rose.

"Gentlemen," he said, "this will be the most magnificent campaign in history. We will annihilate Bolshevism. We will secure Germany's future. We will succeed where Napoleon failed."

A long pause. Then, as if to himself,

"And Stalin will never suspect."

Jodl laid out the history.

"In July last year, preliminary plans were drafted. By December, following our victories in France and the Low Countries, Directive No. 21 was signed—Operation Barbarossa. The goal: swift annihilation of the Red Army before winter sets in."

He traced the arrows on the map:

"Army Group North: Leningrad. Army Group Center: Smolensk, then Moscow. Army Group South: Ukraine, then the Caucasus. Speed is essential. Delay is death."

Then came the debate.

Von Bock spoke first: "Moscow is the prize. It is their nerve center, their industrial heart. If we seize it quickly, the regime collapses."

Von Rundstedt countered: "No. Ukraine is the key. Its resources will cripple them. Starve their war machine, and the rest follows."

Von Leeb, voice calm, added: "Leningrad is their soul. Take it, and morale shatters."

Jodl interjected. "We cannot pursue all objectives. Army Group Center must lead. Moscow must be the focus."

Hitler raised his hand.

"You are all wrong."

Silence.

"The Soviet Union is a rotten structure. Held together by fear. We do not need to take Moscow first—we need to destroy their army. The rest will fall on its own."

Von Bock frowned. "But Mein Führer, where do we strike?"

"Wherever they stand," Hitler snapped. "Encircle. Destroy. Move forward."

Von Rundstedt asked the final question: "And if Moscow resists?"

"Then we adjust."

No room for debate.

CASCADING DIVERGENCE 1941 Lebensraum

Then Hitler laid out the plan:

Army Group North to Leningrad—cut it off, surround it, starve it into submission.

Army Group Center to drive through Smolensk—not focused on reaching Moscow itself, but to destroy Soviet armies en route.

Army Group South through Ukraine—then into the Caucasus to seize the oil fields of Baku and Maikop.

"Moscow," Hitler said, "will fall when we wish it to."

The room was silent.

The men looked at one another, each with thoughts they would never voice aloud. The plan was vast, the gamble immense. But the decision had been made.

There would be no turning back.

RON WOOD

2

A Sleeping Bear
January–March 1941 – Moscow, USSR

I. Kremlin's Veil of Confidence
(January 1941 – Moscow, Kremlin)

Snow blanketed the rooftops of the Kremlin, muting the distant hum of Moscow's nighttime streets. Inside the fortress, where the affairs of the Soviet Union were dictated with cold precision, a small fire crackled in the hearth of Josef Stalin's private office. Despite the warmth, the room remained shrouded in an almost oppressive atmosphere.

At the far end of the chamber, beneath the towering portrait of Lenin, Stalin sat behind a massive mahogany desk, the surface meticulously arranged with intelligence reports, diplomatic briefings, and dossiers marked Секретно (Top Secret). A thin column of smoke drifted upward from the pipe resting between his fingers, curling toward the dim light of the desk lamp. He was hunched slightly forward, his pockmarked face cast in shadow, his dark eyes scanning the latest dispatches from Berlin.

Across from him, seated in stiff wooden chairs, were Vyacheslav Molotov and Lavrentiy Beria, the two most powerful men in the Soviet state after Stalin himself.

Molotov, the Soviet Foreign Minister, sat straight-backed, his bony hands folded in his lap. His thick glasses framed an expression of quiet calculation. A Bolshevik to his core, Molotov had built his career on unwavering loyalty to Stalin, enforcing party doctrine with the same methodical efficiency with which he had negotiated the Molotov-Ribbentrop Pact with Hitler. He believed in that pact—believed, in fact, that the future of Soviet-German relations depended on Stalin's ability to maintain it.

Beria, by contrast, lounged in his chair with a predatory ease. As head of the NKVD, he was a man who thrived on control, his fingers always on the pulse of the Soviet Union's vast network of informants, executioners, and secret police. Unlike Molotov, Beria held no illusions about Hitler's intentions, but he also knew Stalin. And Stalin hated nothing more than being challenged.

The lamplight barely touched the heavy lines around Beria's deep-set eyes. He had seen men disappear overnight for less than suggesting that the Great Leader might be wrong.

Across the table, the General Secretary exhaled a slow plume of smoke. His voice, when it came, was calm but cold.

"And you are certain," Stalin murmured, his gaze still fixed on the reports before him.

Molotov gave a small nod. "Yes, Comrade Stalin. German-Soviet trade continues uninterrupted. Oil, grain, metals—it all flows into the Reich. There is no indication that Hitler intends to break our agreement."

Stalin tapped his pipe against the edge of an ashtray, watching as the embers faded.

CASCADING DIVERGENCE 1941 Lebensraum

"Then why," he asked, "do I keep receiving reports that Germany is moving divisions east?"

Beria smiled thinly, adjusting his spectacles. "Disinformation, most likely. The Germans want us to believe they are stronger than they are. It is in their nature to create paranoia, even where none is warranted."

Molotov nodded in agreement. "It is also possible that these movements are meant for intimidation. If Hitler had intended to attack us, why would he still be so eager to receive our raw materials?"

Stalin considered this, inhaling deeply. He did not trust Hitler—but he trusted logic. Germany was still consolidating its power, reorganizing the territories it had seized in the West. More importantly, Germany relied on Soviet raw materials—without them, the Reich's war machine would grind to a halt.

"Hitler will not be so much a fool as to fight us now," Stalin said, more to himself than to the others. "Not while he needs our oil and steel."

Molotov adjusted his glasses. "That is our assessment as well."

Stalin flicked his pipe into the ashtray and leaned back in his chair.

There would be no war with Germany. Not yet.

II. Warnings Stalin Ignored
(January–February 1941 – Lubyanka, Moscow, USSR)

The corridors of Lubyanka, the NKVD's headquarters, were never truly silent. Footsteps echoed through the marble halls, the sound of boots on stone a constant reminder of the weight of duty and the omnipresent fear that clung to the air. The building's vast offices, dimly lit and lined with towering shelves of classified documents, were filled with the quiet murmur of analysts sifting through intelligence—decrypted messages, intercepted radio transmissions, and reports smuggled out of the Reich by Soviet agents.

The evidence was mounting. Something was happening in Germany.

Major Pavel Sudoplatov, a seasoned analyst with years of experience deciphering enemy movements, sat hunched over his desk, scanning a freshly decoded transmission. His fingers traced the printed lines, his jaw tightening with each phrase. Across the room, his colleague, Lieutenant Yuri Orlov, leaned forward, eyes darting between reports.

"This doesn't add up," Orlov muttered, flipping through a stack of intelligence files.

Sudoplatov exhaled through his nose. "No, it does." He tapped his pen against the paper, frustration flickering in his sharp, tired eyes. "It adds up to war."

The reports were undeniable. The Reich was preparing for something big.

A coded message from Soviet diplomats in Berlin described a troubling pattern—German railway networks were

CASCADING DIVERGENCE 1941 Lebensraum

stockpiling fuel and ammunition along the Soviet border, far more than what was needed for mere "defensive measures."

A separate dispatch from an agent embedded in Poland noted the silent arrival of Wehrmacht divisions, slipping eastward under the cover of routine transfers. Trainloads of troops, armor, and artillery had been spotted disembarking at makeshift supply depots. The Germans were mobilizing, but for what?

When these warnings were compiled and sent to the highest levels of Soviet leadership, the response was eerily familiar.

Silence—or worse.

The official line from the Kremlin was unwavering—Germany was a strategic partner. The nonaggression pact between Molotov and Ribbentrop remained in place. Trade agreements for oil, grain, and steel continued as scheduled. And Stalin, above all, had dismissed the idea of a German betrayal outright.

"These reports are exaggerations," Stalin had scoffed at a recent meeting, his tone flat, his expression unreadable. "Or lies, meant to turn us against Hitler."

The NKVD officers knew what that meant.

The General Secretary had made up his mind.

The truth no longer mattered

Inside Lubyanka's intelligence offices, the atmosphere grew heavier. Analysts who once meticulously compiled warnings now hesitated, second-guessing their own findings. If Stalin refused to acknowledge the evidence, then what good was reporting it?

Sudoplatov closed the file on his desk. Another report that wouldn't be acted upon. Another warning ignored.

He turned to Orlov. "How much do we include in today's report?"

Orlov hesitated. "If we send everything, it could be seen as alarmism."

"Or worse," Sudoplatov added darkly.

They both knew what happened to those accused of spreading "defeatist propaganda." The gulags. A bullet in the back of the head. A quiet disappearance.

Some intelligence officers, already frustrated with the Kremlin's rejection of their work, began self-censoring. If the General Secretary refused to believe Germany was preparing for war, then what good would it do to tell him otherwise?

One senior NKVD officer, when asked why he had altered his assessment of German troop movements, simply replied:

"Better to be wrong with Stalin than right without him."

III. Dangerous Complacency
(February–March 1941 – Soviet Western Military Districts, USSR)

At forward Soviet garrisons, reports of German activity along the border grew more frequent, yet no reinforcements arrived, no new directives were issued from Moscow. Along

CASCADING DIVERGENCE 1941 Lebensraum

the vast Soviet frontier, entire divisions remained scattered in peacetime formations, unfortified and vulnerable.

- Soviet airfields remained densely packed with aircraft, with no effort to disperse them in case of bombing.
- Supply depots sat dangerously close to the border, making them easy targets for a sudden attack.
- Red Army officers who raised concerns were dismissed as alarmists.

At an officer's briefing in early March, General Dmitry Pavlov, commander of the Western Special Military District, expressed concern about the lack of fortifications along his sector of the border. When his report reached the Kremlin, Stalin was furious.

"Enough of this defeatist talk!" he reportedly snapped. "If I hear any more nonsense about a German attack, there will be consequences!"

IV. Germans Observe Soviet Inaction
(March 1941 – German-Soviet Border, Wehrmacht Intelligence Reports)

The morning light cast a glow across the open fields of Eastern Europe, stretching toward the Soviet frontier. From a vantage point on a low ridgeline, Colonel Reinhard Gehlen, one of Germany's top intelligence officers, lowered his binoculars in disbelief.

"Nothing," he muttered. "Absolutely nothing."

He handed the binoculars to Major Walter Schellenberg, an SS intelligence operative assigned to monitor Soviet military behavior.

Schellenberg took a long look, scanning the rows of Soviet border fortifications—or rather, the absence of them. The Red Army outposts below were completely unaltered, their wooden watchtowers still manned by lazily pacing sentries, their trenches half-dug and abandoned to the winter frost.

But it wasn't just the lack of fortifications that baffled them.

It was the entire Soviet military posture.

For months, the Wehrmacht had been steadily building up along the border—3.2 million German soldiers, their Panzer divisions hidden in forests, their supply convoys rumbling eastward under the cover of night. They were preparing for war.

But the Soviets?

They were doing—nothing.

By midday, Luftwaffe reconnaissance flights returned with more detailed reports.

The photographs and radio intercepts delivered to Army High Command (OKH) painted a picture of sheer Soviet complacency.

- Soviet airfields remained untouched—no dispersal of aircraft, no camouflage, no visible preparations.
- Railway hubs showed no signs of troop reinforcements or logistical buildup.

CASCADING DIVERGENCE 1941 Lebensraum

- Border garrisons maintained their standard peacetime patrols—unchanged, unaware.

In a secure communications tent, Major Helmut Meyer, an intelligence officer with the Abwehr, sifted through the latest aerial imagery with General Franz Halder, Chief of the Army General Staff.

Halder leaned over a freshly developed reconnaissance photograph, his gloved hand tracing a cluster of Soviet fighter planes lined neatly along a runway in Brest-Litovsk—rows of MiG-3s and I-16s, vulnerable and unmoved, as if no one in the Soviet command had even considered the possibility of a first strike.

He shook his head in disbelief. "They haven't even repositioned their aircraft," Halder said. "When the first wave of Stukas comes in, it will be over before they can start their engines."

Meyer nodded. "It's almost too easy."

Beyond the Luftwaffe's findings, the Wehrmacht's ground intelligence confirmed an equally shocking reality—no defensive mobilization, no increase in troop numbers, no heightened alert status.

At a forward listening post, German radio operators intercepted Soviet military chatter.

"Routine patrols remain unchanged. No new orders from Moscow."

The radio operators glanced at one another, bewildered.

"Their own officers are asking for guidance, and Moscow is ignoring them," one of them muttered.

Even German spies embedded in Soviet-occupied Poland and Ukraine reported that Red Army officers remained completely unprepared for war. Some had even dismissed rumors of an imminent German invasion as "propaganda" from enemies of the state.

At a secure command post near Rastenburg, Field Marshal Fedor von Bock, commander of Army Group Center, studied these latest intelligence reports with mounting excitement.

He turned to his staff and spoke with uncharacteristic glee.

"They are asleep," von Bock said. "They see nothing, hear nothing, expect nothing."

When the intelligence reports were compiled and presented in Berlin, they made their way to Adolf Hitler himself.

As he sat in his war room at the Reich Chancellery, reading the summaries from the Wehrmacht, Luftwaffe, and Abwehr, his mood brightened.

He placed the report down and looked around at his gathered generals—Keitel, Jodl, Göring, Halder.

"They have done nothing," he said, a slow grin creeping across his face.

"The moment we strike, they will fall apart."

At the German forward bases along the border, the final preparations for Operation Barbarossa continued.

CASCADING DIVERGENCE 1941 Lebensraum

Trains carrying fuel, ammunition, and troops moved under the cover of darkness.

Panzers sat hidden in the forests of East Prussia and occupied Poland, their engines cold—but waiting.

Luftwaffe squadrons ran final drills, their pilots sharpening their attack patterns for the opening blitz.

Everything was in place.

And across the border, the Red Army remained completely blind to the storm that was about to descend upon them.

The trap was set—Barbarossa was coming.

RON WOOD

3

The Ruse
February–April 1941, German-Soviet Border

I. Illusion of Defense
(February 1941 – Wehrmacht Forward Command, East Prussia)

Along the German-Soviet frontier, a carefully staged illusion was unfolding. Barbed-wire fences stretched along the ridgeline, their sharp edges catching the pale glint of the winter sun. German engineers moved deliberately, hammering wooden stakes into the frozen ground, affixing signs marked in bold, black letters: *Achtung! Minen!* (Warning! Mines!). Beyond them, soldiers patrolled in slow, deliberate circuits, their boots crunching against the frost-coated earth—not the tense strides of men preparing for war, but the routine, measured steps of a force settling into defense. It was all meant to be seen, to be reported back to Moscow. And the Soviets were watching.

On an elevated embankment overlooking the border, Colonel Erich Marcks peered through a pair of Zeiss field glasses, scanning the orchestrated performance unfolding below. His breath fogged against the lenses, momentarily obscuring his view, but even without them, he could see the scene playing out exactly as planned.

Hundreds of German engineers and infantrymen bustled along the apparent defensive lines—a carefully staged deception. Earthworks were being dug, timber palisades were erected, and barbed wire stretched in redundant loops around supposed strongpoints. Here and there, dummy artillery positions were set up, their "guns" nothing more than painted wooden logs mounted on wheels, perfectly positioned for any Soviet reconnaissance patrols to observe from across the border.

Marcks lowered his binoculars, exhaling sharply.

"Make sure they see everything," he muttered to the officer beside him. "Every last trench, every last minefield."

Major Hasso von Manteuffel, standing at his side, adjusted the fur collar of his Wehrmacht greatcoat and gave a knowing smile. The illusion of a defensive posture had to be perfect.

"They'll see it, Colonel," Manteuffel assured him. "Our patrol routes have been adjusted to 'accidentally' allow them just the right glimpses."

Marcks nodded. Nothing was left to chance.

Down below, soldiers moved with well-rehearsed precision, pretending to fortify positions that would never be used in combat.

A group of engineers worked at the base of a shallow trench, their shovels biting into the frozen earth with a rhythm designed to be seen, not completed.

A few yards away, a group of riflemen moved in synchronized patrols, their movements deliberately slow and predictable—not the alert pacing of soldiers expecting battle, but the calculated motions of men who wanted to be seen.

Farther along the line, a squad of German soldiers hammered wooden stakes into the frozen ground, affixing signs marked in bold, black letters:

Achtung! Minen! (Warning! Mines!)

Marcks smirked.

"Are those real mines?" he asked, gesturing toward the warning signs.

Manteuffel chuckled, shaking his head. "Some. But most are wooden dummies—hollow casings, filled with nothing but air." He glanced at the carefully arranged defensive positions below. "Convincing enough?"

Marcks surveyed the landscape once more. It was a masterpiece of deception—a fortress that would crumble like dust the moment German troops surged eastward.

"Convincing enough," Marcks echoed.

Everything had been planned to perfection. The Soviets would see exactly what Berlin wanted them to see—a Germany that was preparing to defend, not attack.

This was deception on an industrial scale, an elaborate ruse designed to lull Stalin into complacency.

And across the border, Soviet intelligence officers were falling for it.

II. Feeding Stalin's Delusions
(March 1941 – German Embassy, Moscow)

The German Embassy in Moscow stood as an island of diplomacy in a sea of paranoia. Thick stone walls and uniformed guards offered little protection from the ever-present eyes of the NKVD, whose agents lurked in the alleys and corridors of Soviet bureaucracy, their whispers carrying suspicions and secrets alike.

Inside the embassy, Ambassador Friedrich-Werner von der Schulenburg adjusted the cuffs of his pristine uniform, exhaling quietly before stepping into his car. The invitation—or rather, the summons—to the Soviet Foreign Ministry had been expected.

Molotov had questions.

Schulenburg knew the answers had already been written for him in Berlin.

The drive through Moscow was uneventful, though the city had taken on a certain grayness, a weight that had nothing to do with the still-lingering frost of winter. Fear and obedience were visible in the rigid postures of workers along the boulevards, their eyes cast downward even as the limousine of the German ambassador passed them.

By the time Schulenburg stepped into Molotov's chamber, the tension was already there, waiting.

Molotov sat behind a wooden desk, his hands folded with calculated stillness, his steel-rimmed glasses perched low on his nose. He did not rise to greet the German ambassador.

Schulenburg knew better than to take offense.

CASCADING DIVERGENCE 1941 Lebensraum

"Herr Schulenburg," Molotov said, his tone clipped, "Soviet intelligence has noted increased German troop movements near the border. I assume there is an explanation?"

There was no preamble, no exchange of formalities.

Schulenburg smiled, an expression of carefully measured reassurance.

"Minister Molotov, I assure you, there is nothing to be concerned about," he said smoothly. "Routine maneuvers, nothing more. The shifting of our logistics network, a necessary redistribution of resources." He paused before delivering the next part, ensuring it sounded like an inconvenient truth rather than a well-crafted fiction. "In fact, Reichsmarschall Göring is quite frustrated with the state of our fuel reserves. It has forced us to relocate certain supply depots."

Molotov studied him, his expression unreadable, though Schulenburg could see the gears turning behind his cold, bureaucratic stare. He was analyzing, calculating—but not doubting.

Finally, the Soviet Foreign Minister leaned back in his chair.

"We have also noticed new fortifications along the German-Soviet frontier," Molotov said, voice deliberately neutral. "Surely, you are not expecting trouble?"

Schulenburg shrugged lightly, as if the notion was entirely unnecessary.

"Not at all," he said. "Our leadership is simply taking precautions. In times of uncertainty, one can never be too careful."

Molotov exhaled slowly, his fingers tapping against the wooden desk.

He had already received confirmation of this from his own intelligence operatives. German reconnaissance positions, defensive trench networks, even the visible relocation of supply lines—all pointed toward a Germany that was protecting itself, not preparing for war.

And, most crucially, Stalin wanted to believe it.

Molotov nodded once, finally conceding.

"Very well," he said, pressing his fingertips together. "We see no reason for concern, then."

Schulenburg's smile deepened, but only for a fraction of a second.

The deception was complete.

III. Controlling What the Soviets See
(March 1941 – German-Soviet Border, Occupied Poland)

The late winter air hung heavy over the railway junction outside Lublin, Poland. The skeletal remains of the previous autumn's grass poked through patches of frost-covered mud, and a low mist curled between the steel tracks. Somewhere in the distance, the whistle of a departing train echoed through the countryside, swallowed almost immediately by the mechanical roar of engines idling on the platform.

Amidst the controlled chaos of railway workers and Wehrmacht engineers, Captain Otto Skorzeny stood watching. His presence was an anomaly among the standard-

CASCADING DIVERGENCE 1941 Lebensraum

issue uniforms. Tall, broad-shouldered, and exuding a quiet menace, the Austrian officer was already gaining a reputation in the Reich's growing network of unconventional warfare experts. Though he had yet to achieve the notoriety that would one day make him infamous, his orders came from the highest levels, and he was very good at following them.

Tonight, his mission was simple but critical—make sure the Soviets saw exactly what Berlin wanted them to see.

Trains were moving east in massive numbers. But not all of them carried troops. Not all of them carried weapons. That was the key to the deception.

Skorzeny turned toward a nervous-looking lieutenant, who was overseeing the loading of several cargo wagons onto an outbound train. The men were working quickly, hauling timber planks, steel beams, crates of barbed wire, and empty fuel drums into the cars. The lieutenant snapped to attention when he noticed Skorzeny watching.

"Captain, these are the last of the marked wagons. Scheduled to leave within the hour," the lieutenant reported, his voice clipped with efficiency.

Skorzeny gave a slow nod. "Good," he murmured.

His gaze drifted beyond the platform, toward the shadowy ridges on the far side of the railway yard. The Soviets were out there, watching. He was sure of it. They had been watching for months.

Soviet intelligence had carefully placed observers all along the border, posing as Polish railway workers, displaced civilians, or even neutral foreign diplomats. They watched the German supply lines, studying every movement of train schedules, fuel shipments, artillery transfers.

The information they smuggled back to Moscow was invaluable—at least, it would have been, if only they were seeing the truth.

But what the Soviets did not know—what they could never be allowed to know—was that the real troop movements were happening elsewhere.

Under the cover of darkness, hundreds of miles away, the true battle formations of the Wehrmacht were shifting eastward. Elite Panzer divisions and mechanized infantry units, carefully concealed within forests and dispersed across hidden staging areas, avoided the major railway hubs entirely.

Instead, the Soviets saw what they expected to see:

- Rows of train cars filled with construction materials—evidence of "border fortifications", not preparation for an invasion.

- Trucks carrying supplies toward border outposts—enough to maintain the illusion of a defensive posture.

- Fencing projects, watchtowers, and trenches being dug—all carefully staged, but ultimately, meaningless.

And yet, it was enough to reinforce Stalin's delusion that Germany was not preparing for an offensive operation.

Skorzeny turned back to the lieutenant. "Make sure the Soviets get a good look at this one," he said, gesturing toward the train. "And remind our men to keep the floodlights on."

CASCADING DIVERGENCE 1941 Lebensraum

The lieutenant hesitated for only a moment before nodding. "Understood, Captain."

The Germans wanted Soviet reconnaissance to see the movement of construction materials. Wanted them to take notes, report to Moscow, and confirm what Stalin already believed—that Germany was fortifying its defenses, not assembling for the largest invasion in history.

Somewhere beyond the ridgeline, a pair of Soviet binoculars caught the faint glow of floodlights illuminating the harmless-looking supply train.

The observer scribbled a few notes in his worn leather notebook, then disappeared back into the night, unknowingly carrying exactly the message Berlin intended to send.

IV. Soviet High Command Does Nothing
(April 1941 – Kremlin, Moscow)

The air inside the Stavka conference chamber was thick with the acrid stench of cigarette smoke and stale sweat, mingling with the heavy musk of overworked uniforms. A haze clung to the dimly lit room, where flickering lamps illuminated the gathering of the Soviet Union's most powerful military minds—all sitting in tense deliberation.

Maps and intelligence reports lay sprawled out, covered in hastily scrawled annotations—circles, arrows, figures, all trying to make sense of the growing unease gripping Moscow. Dozens of reports, all pointing to the same conclusion.

Yet, no one was acting on them.

Marshal Georgy Zhukov, Chief of the General Staff, sat stiffly in his chair, his expression hardened by frustration. He had always been a soldier first—a man of action, not words—and yet here he was, forced into endless meetings, watching power shift not by military logic, but by political stubbornness.

Clearing his throat, he straightened slightly and addressed the men seated around him.

"Comrades, we have received multiple reports of German troop concentrations near our western border," Zhukov began, his voice measured but firm. "Yet we see no indication of offensive preparations."

The statement hung in the air, waiting for someone—anyone—to challenge it.

Across from him, Marshal Semyon Timoshenko, Stalin's Commissar of Defense, exhaled slowly, rubbing his forehead as if he were explaining something for the tenth time.

"Comrade Stalin has already spoken on this," he said flatly. "The Germans are not preparing to attack. They are fortifying their side of the border, likely fearing that we may move first."

A murmur of agreement rippled through the table.

Zhukov's brow furrowed. He had read the same intelligence reports, studied the same aerial reconnaissance photographs. The Germans were moving divisions, establishing logistical hubs, reinforcing supply lines.

He leaned forward, his knuckles pressing against the table.

CASCADING DIVERGENCE 1941 Lebensraum

"And if we are wrong?" Zhukov asked pointedly. "If the Germans are masking an invasion?"

Timoshenko barely looked up from his papers, waving a dismissive hand. "We are not wrong," he said simply.

Zhukov's jaw tightened.

At the head of the table, a shadow moved.

Seated in his usual position, Josef Stalin, the General Secretary, the Vozhd, the Great Helmsman, sat in complete silence.

He had not spoken throughout the entire discussion. He had simply listened, smoking his signature pipe, his pockmarked face unreadable beneath the dim lighting. His dark eyes, sharp as daggers, studied the room, watching the unspoken tension play out among his generals.

Then, slowly, Stalin lifted a single hand and tapped his index finger against his desk.

A sound so soft, and yet in this room, it might as well have been a gunshot.

The murmuring stopped immediately.

Every head turned toward him.

"You are being too paranoid, Zhukov," Stalin said, his voice low and unbothered, his gaze unwavering.

The words were final.

"If Hitler wanted war, he would not be begging for our oil," Stalin continued, exhaling a plume of blue-gray smoke from his pipe. "He would not be buying our steel. He needs us."

Silence.

For a moment, Zhukov thought of arguing.

But then, his eyes met Stalin's.

And he understood.

There was no room for doubt.

Not in Stalin's world.

Zhukov sat back slowly, biting his tongue.

Timoshenko relaxed. Others leaned back, the moment of tension passing like a storm cloud drifting away.

Nothing would be done.

The Soviets would take no action at all.

V. Confirmation the Ruse Has Worked
(April 1941 – OKH Headquarters, Zossen, Germany)

The air inside German Army High Command (OKH) Headquarters buzzed with conversation. The war room, a vast chamber lined with maps and radio equipment, was the nerve center of the Wehrmacht's strategic planning. Officers moved briskly between desks piled with reports, typewritten orders, and reconnaissance photographs spread across polished wooden surfaces.

CASCADING DIVERGENCE 1941 Lebensraum

At the center of it all, General Franz Halder stood beside a massive operational map, his gloved finger tracing the long, winding curve of the Soviet frontier—from the Baltic to the Black Sea. He had studied this map countless times, but today, it looked different. Not as an enemy stronghold, but as an unlocked door waiting to be kicked open.

The room hummed with quiet tension.

The latest intelligence reports had arrived, delivered by Luftwaffe couriers and Wehrmacht reconnaissance teams stationed along the border. Officers examined the details, verifying them over and over, confirming what seemed almost too good to be true.

Field Marshal Walther von Brauchitsch, the Commander-in-Chief of the Army, stepped forward, arms crossed. His piercing blue eyes scanned the map. A man of discipline and precision, he had seen many strategic opportunities in war—but this one left him astonished.

"They are doing nothing," he murmured, almost in disbelief. The Soviets' inaction seemed too absurd to be real.

Halder nodded, a faint smirk forming at the corner of his mouth.

"They are blind."

The reports laid it out in stark detail:

Soviet border positions remained unchanged. No troop movement. No defensive shifts. No indication that Moscow suspected what was coming.

No reinforcements. Soviet divisions, still in peacetime formations, were spread too thin—exposed and vulnerable.

Airfields were untouched. German reconnaissance confirmed Soviet fighter planes neatly lined up in rows, sitting ducks for an attack. No camouflage. No dispersal. No defensive preparations.

Railway networks showed no signs of mobilization. Troop transports that should have been rushing reinforcements eastward remained empty. The mighty Red Army stood still, oblivious to the impending storm.

A courier entered, the swastika-emblazoned armband on his uniform catching the lamplight. He marched briskly toward the map table, snapped to attention, and handed Halder a sealed Luftwaffe communiqué.

Halder broke the seal, scanning the message. His expression sharpened.

"The Luftwaffe confirms no Soviet defensive buildup," he announced. "Stalin still believes we are preparing to defend, not attack."

A stunned silence filled the room.

Von Brauchitsch, normally composed, exhaled sharply. His disbelief was evident.

"*Mein Gott...* It actually worked."

Halder slipped the message into his breast pocket and turned back to the map. The Soviet defenses stretched before him like an invitation—open, unprepared. He pictured what

CASCADING DIVERGENCE 1941 Lebensraum

would soon unfold: divisions in retreat, cities in flames, Moscow within reach.

"They have left their throat exposed," he said, his voice low and deliberate.

The officers leaned in, drawn to the gravity of his words.

"When the time comes, we will strike."

Halder clasped his hands behind his back, his gaze cold, assured.

RON WOOD

CASCADING DIVERGENCE 1941 Lebensraum

4

Stalin's Growing Overconfidence
March–April 1941 – Moscow, USSR

I. The Man Who Trusted No One
(March 1941 – Kremlin, Stalin's Office)

Josef Stalin sat behind his vast mahogany desk, a fortress of polished wood and cold calculation. The dim glow of his desk lamp cast long shadows across the stacks of intelligence reports, some still sealed, others opened but discarded—as if their warnings were unworthy of his time. Outside, the Kremlin walls loomed over Moscow, shielding the heart of Soviet power from the waking city beyond.

Inside this chamber, where life and death were decided with the stroke of a pen, the atmosphere was suffocating. The fire crackled in the hearth, but the warmth did not reach the men seated before Stalin. They shifted uncomfortably, their expressions carefully neutral, their postures rigid.

Across the desk, Lavrentiy Beria, head of the NKVD, lounged with deceptive ease. His round, soft features masked the ruthless cunning that had built his empire of informants, prisons, and executioners. His hands were clasped in his lap, his smirk faint but ever-present. To his left, Marshal Semyon Timoshenko, the Commissar of Defense, sat uncomfortably upright, his uniform stiff, his face drawn. Unlike Beria, he was genuinely troubled.

Across from them, Stalin tapped two fingers against the desk, a slow, deliberate rhythm. The sound was almost hypnotic, filling the silence with an unspoken message—he was thinking, and they would wait.

At last, he spoke.

"I have been hearing the same story for months now," Stalin muttered, his tone unreadable. He reached for a dossier at the top of the pile, flipping it open without looking at the words inside. "First, it was that the Germans were sending reconnaissance planes too frequently. Then, that they were reinforcing supply depots. Now, you tell me they are massing troops?"

He exhaled a slow plume of pipe smoke, letting it curl upward, lingering before vanishing into the dimness above.

Timoshenko hesitated, then leaned forward. "Comrade Stalin, these are not minor movements. Entire divisions are redeploying east. Our intelligence suggests that Germany is increasing its strength near the border. This could be preparation for—"

A sharp wave of Stalin's hand cut him off. The movement was small, but in the Kremlin, such gestures carried weight.

"For what?" Stalin's voice was soft, yet razor-edged.

A tense pause followed.

CASCADING DIVERGENCE 1941 Lebensraum

Timoshenko, his throat dry, forced himself to meet Stalin's gaze. He had commanded men in battle, but there was no greater battlefield than this room. He knew the price of hesitation—and the cost of speaking too soon.

Finally, he answered, carefully.

"An attack."

The room was silent, save for the distant ticking of the ornate clock mounted on the wall.

Then, Beria chuckled softly.

It was not the laugh of amusement, but of mockery, a man relishing the moment when someone else would bear Stalin's wrath. He shook his head slightly, his fingers interlacing with slow precision, his voice smooth as silk.

"And what would be the purpose of that, Marshal?" Beria murmured. His glasses reflected the lamplight, obscuring his eyes, but the amusement was clear in his tone. "Do you really think Hitler would be foolish enough to strike while we are feeding his nation?"

He let the question hang, savoring the moment before answering it himself.

"Without our oil, his tanks will rust in place."

Stalin's expression did not change, but something in the room did. The air grew heavier, as if the oxygen itself had been drawn away, leaving only the thick weight of unspoken judgment.

Slowly, he leaned back in his chair, pipe held between his fingers. His eyes, half-lidded, locked onto Timoshenko's.

"Exactly," Stalin murmured. "Hitler is not a fool."

He stroked his mustache thoughtfully, as if the conversation were already over. A verdict had been reached.

The warnings would go unheeded.

Beria's smirk widened slightly. Timoshenko, though silent, felt his stomach turn. He had seen men disappear for less than contradicting Stalin's instincts.

And Stalin's instincts, for now, had convinced him that war was impossible.

II. Warnings Stalin Did Not Want to Hear
(March 1941 – NKVD Intelligence Division, Lubyanka, Moscow)

The corridors of Lubyanka, the dreaded NKVD headquarters, pulsed with quiet urgency. Footsteps echoed through the marble halls. Documents rustled as they were ferried from one dimly lit office to another. Conversations were hushed, words chosen carefully—everyone knew that speaking too loudly could end careers. Or lives.

In a basement analysis room, a single desk lamp cast an uneven light over scattered intelligence reports. Papers lay spread across the table like a puzzle no one dared to solve. The air was thick with the scent of ink, sweat, and stale tobacco—an oppressive reminder of endless hours spent deciphering messages no one wanted to read.

At the center of it all, Major Pavel Sudoplatov rubbed his temples, exhaustion pressing into his bones. He had spent weeks tracking a pattern that no longer seemed coincidental—German troop movements, railway reinforcements, fuel stockpiles accumulating in the east. Something was happening.

And yet, no one wanted to hear it.

Exhaling sharply, he grabbed a newly decrypted report, scanned its contents, and slid it across the desk to his superior, Colonel Fyodor Fedotov.

"Another railway reinforcement order," Sudoplatov muttered. His voice was controlled, but an unmistakable edge lurked beneath it. "They're expanding rail capacity toward the border. More trains, every week. They're preparing for something—this isn't routine."

Fedotov barely glanced at the paper. With a practiced motion, he shut the folder and pushed it back onto the growing pile of ignored warnings.

"File it with the others," he said, his voice flat.

Sudoplatov stared at him. "Sir, we have to bring this to the General Secretary. The signs are—"

The scrape of Fedotov's chair cut him off.

In an instant, the colonel was on his feet, palms flat on the table, leaning in until his face was inches from Sudoplatov's. His expression remained neutral, but his eyes carried a warning sharper than any blade.

"You think I don't know?" Fedotov's voice was low, barely more than a whisper. But the menace in it was unmistakable.

Across the room, the other analysts froze.

Fedotov straightened slightly but did not step back. "Do you want to end up in a gulag?" His tone remained calm, almost conversational. Then, softer, deadlier: "Or worse?"

The silence thickened, a suffocating weight pressing against every man in the room. No one spoke. No one moved.

Sudoplatov swallowed hard, his mouth suddenly dry.

"Comrade Stalin has decided that Hitler will not attack," Fedotov continued, his voice cold and final. "Which means we have decided that Hitler will not attack. Do I make myself clear?"

Sudoplatov clenched his jaw. A response was required, and the wrong one could cost him his career—or his life.

After a tense moment, he gave a stiff, reluctant nod.

Fedotov held his gaze a moment longer, then smoothed the front of his uniform. Without another word, he turned on his heel and strode out of the room, the heavy door swinging shut behind him.

The analysts exhaled, exchanging brief, uneasy glances. But no one spoke.

With a measured hand, Sudoplatov reached forward and gathered the report, its contents damning—but now worthless.

Without ceremony, he pushed it aside, adding it to the growing pile of truths buried under fear.

CASCADING DIVERGENCE 1941 Lebensraum

III. Fate of the Red Army
(April 1941 – Western Military District, Soviet Borderlands)

The Western Military District stretched across the Soviet frontier, vast but unprepared. To the west, beyond the Bug River, the Wehrmacht was gathering. Hidden in the forests of Poland and Romania, German divisions stood ready, waiting for the order to strike.

Yet within the Red Army, there was no urgency. No alarms. No preparations.

At a dusty airfield near Brest-Litovsk, everything was routine. The morning sun reflected off the metal fuselages of Soviet fighter planes. Their red-star insignias stood out against the pale blue sky. They were lined up in perfect rows, exposed, easy targets should enemy bombers arrive.

Inside a small command tent, junior officers huddled around a worn wooden table. Cigarette smoke drifted through the air. A lieutenant traced a line across a weathered map, his brow furrowed.

"Orders?" he asked, looking toward his superior.

Across from him, Colonel Anatoly Gusarov leaned back in his chair. He was in his forties, hardened by years of service. But he showed no tension, no sign that war was coming.

"No changes," he said, flicking ash into a tin tray. His voice was calm, though there was a trace of irritation—not at the Germans, but at the endless rumors of war. "No new deployments. No maneuvers. We stay at our posts and wait for orders from Moscow."

The lieutenant frowned. "We're sitting ducks."

Gusarov shot him a look.

"We do nothing without orders," he said firmly. "And Moscow says the Germans are not a threat."

The words hung over the room.

Outside, the distant hum of an approaching aircraft made some heads turn—but it was nothing unusual. Another Soviet patrol plane, finishing its daily reconnaissance. The same report would come in, as always: All quiet. No unusual German activity.

Gusarov crushed his cigarette into the tray and stood.

"That's all," he said. "Back to your stations."

The officers saluted, but the tension remained.

As the lieutenant left, he glanced one last time at the open hangar doors. The morning light spilled onto the silent, motionless rows of Soviet fighter planes.

They were waiting.

Exposed.

Helpless.

IV. Germans Prepare to Strike
(April 1941 – OKH Headquarters, Zossen, Germany)

The Wehrmacht's headquarters buzzed with activity. Maps lined the walls. Typewriters clicked. Germany's top military officers studied the latest intelligence from the Eastern Front.

CASCADING DIVERGENCE 1941 Lebensraum

The reports were shocking.

The Soviet Union, Hitler's greatest enemy, was doing nothing.

No reinforcements.

No defensive positions.

Airfields left completely exposed.

For weeks, aerial reconnaissance had shown the same results. Soviet forces remained static. Their defenses were unchanged. Even their airfields were packed with aircraft that had not been dispersed. Stalin seemed unwilling to acknowledge reality.

At the center of the room, General Franz Halder, Chief of the Army General Staff, stood with his arms crossed. His sharp eyes scanned the latest intelligence reports. Silence filled the chamber.

"They are blind," one officer muttered.

Halder set down his report with a thud.

"No," he corrected. "Worse than blind. They refuse to see."

The Soviet high command, responsible for defending a nation of nearly 200 million, was frozen in denial. Their military was unprepared. Their strategy was nonexistent. If the Wehrmacht struck now, it would be like cutting through air.

Before anyone could speak, the doors swung open. A courier entered, his boots clicking on the polished floor. He carried a sealed communiqué stamped with the insignia of the Abwehr—Germany's military intelligence service.

Halder took it, unfolded the paper, and read quickly. Then, he smirked.

"Stalin has dismissed all intelligence warnings," he announced. "He believes we will not attack."

A ripple of disbelief passed through the room.

By the strategy table, Field Marshal Walther von Brauchitsch, Commander-in-Chief of the Army, exhaled slowly.

"Mein Gott." His voice was quiet. "They've done nothing."

The truth settled over them.

The feared Red Army had left itself wide open. Stalin's refusal to act had given Germany a priceless advantage.

Halder folded the message and placed it on the table. He straightened.

"Then," he said, his voice calm, "they deserve what's coming."

The order was clear.

Operation Barbarossa—the largest invasion in history—was ready.

5

The Calm Before the Storm

Late April–May 1941, German-Soviet Borderlands

I. Under Maps and Shadows
(late April 1941 – Wehrmacht Forward Headquarters, Rastenburg, East Prussia)

The underground war room of the Wehrmacht's forward command hummed with restless energy. The atmosphere was thick with unspoken tension—not of doubt, but of anticipation, the kind that came just before the world changed.

Field Marshal Fedor von Bock, commander of Army Group Center, stood at the edge of the strategy table, his gloved fingers pressing against the massive operations map before him. His lean, angular face remained expressionless, but in the glow of the overhead lamps, his sharp eyes betrayed a rare intensity. He had spent his entire career in war—Poland, France, the Low Countries—but never had he faced a campaign of this magnitude.

This was not merely an invasion.

It was the largest military operation in history.

Operation Barbarossa—the final war against Bolshevism, the drive to the East, the war of annihilation—was about to begin.

Beside von Bock, General Hermann Hoth, commander of the 3rd Panzer Group, leaned forward, his hand tracing thick red arrows that cut through Soviet territory. His gaze was focused, his posture radiating the kind of confidence that only men who had mastered Blitzkrieg could possess.

"If we break them early," Hoth muttered, his voice low, certain, "nothing will stop us before Moscow."

Von Bock exhaled sharply. His steely gaze remained on the map.

"If," he echoed.

Hoth's certainty was infectious, but von Bock had seen too much war to indulge in optimism. The Soviets were an unknown quantity—a vast army that, though crude in training and outdated in tactics, had an unforgiving depth. Victory would come, yes—but at what cost?

Across the room, Field Marshal Walther von Brauchitsch, Commander-in-Chief of the Army, remained silent, his gaze unreadable as he listened. Unlike some of the men gathered here, he was no political zealot. He understood the true nature of this war—not one of German survival, but of Hitler's ambition, a war that had been forced upon the army, one that would stretch the Wehrmacht beyond anything it had endured before.

CASCADING DIVERGENCE 1941 Lebensraum

And if Barbarossa failed, it would not be Hitler who paid the price.

It would be them. The generals. The officers. The men standing in this room.

Von Brauchitsch let out a breath. He knew he had only one duty left—to ensure that failure was not an option.

"We will smash them so quickly they won't know what hit them," Hoth said, his confidence unshaken.

Von Brauchitsch studied him for a long moment, his expression betraying nothing. Then, finally, he gave a small nod.

"See to it, General."

A soft knock sounded at the door to the war room. An adjutant stepped in, handing von Bock a sealed communiqué bearing the OKH insignia. He read it swiftly, eyes narrowing slightly as he handed it to Hoth beside him.

"Rommel's assignment is confirmed," von Bock said, folding the paper crisply.

Hoth raised an eyebrow. "He's coming east?"

Von Bock nodded. "With Britain out of the war, North Africa no longer requires his presence. The Führer wants him here—spearheading a breakout through the Pripyat Marshes to swing north of Smolensk."

There was a moment of silence.

"Rommel in the east," Hoth mused. "The Soviets won't know what hit them."

The room's strategic map was adjusted. Now, three distinct thrusts from Army Group Center stood out—Guderian to the south, Hoth to the north, and Rommel threading the needle between them, tasked with executing aggressive maneuver warfare deep into Soviet lines.

Each general brought a different tempo to the battlefield:

Heinz Guderian, the father of Blitzkrieg, methodical and relentless.

Hermann Hoth, precise and adaptable, a master of flank strikes.

And now, Erwin Rommel, unpredictable and daring, a gambler with a general's mind.

Together, under von Bock's command, they would drive a wedge into the Soviet heartland. Moscow was the objective—but destruction of the Red Army en route was the true goal.

Von Bock allowed himself a rare thought:

If this team of commanders couldn't break Stalin, perhaps no one could.

The officers dispersed, their boots echoing against the concrete as they left the chamber.

Above them, beyond the thick walls of the Führer's Wolf's Lair, a war machine three million men strong was waiting.

The invasion of the Soviet Union was no longer a plan.

It was an unstoppable reality.

CASCADING DIVERGENCE 1941 Lebensraum

II. Predator at the Gates
(April–May 1941, German-Occupied Poland and Romania)

The borderlands from the Baltic to the Black Sea held their breath, silent beneath a sky painted in deep twilight. Hidden among the dense forests, nestled in sleepy villages, and crammed into railway stations where no train dared move, more than 3.2 million German soldiers waited. Some sat beside their vehicles, their boots resting on packed rations, helmets tucked beneath their arms. Others sharpened knives, rechecked their rifles, or smoked in tense silence. Officers murmured in low voices, finalizing orders that would soon set the world on fire. In the hush of the waiting army, the weight of history pressed down upon them all. Barbarossa was no longer just a plan—it was inevitable.

Under the cover of moonless nights, armored convoys moved like phantoms, their heavy treads wrapped in thick tarps to muffle their passage. Trainloads of fuel, munitions, and provisions rumbled eastward, slipping into hidden depots that had been constructed over the preceding months. The Luftwaffe, too, had taken its place in the great deception—fighter squadrons relocated under the pretense of routine training exercises, while bombers sat idle on airfields, their lethal cargo waiting to be unleashed.

At a staging area near Lublin, Poland, General Heinz Guderian stood atop a command half-track, his eyes scanning the horizon, where row upon row of Panzer III and Panzer IV tanks stretched across the open fields. Their dark camouflage blended into the landscape, their steel hulls reflecting the last glimmers of a dying sun.

Down below, tank crews lounged against their machines, sharing cigarettes, tightening bolts, and checking the gears that would soon carry them deep into Soviet territory. Some played cards, their laughter subdued but present—the nervous ease of men who knew their fate was measured in kilometers, not years.

General Erich Hoepner, standing beside Guderian, let out a slow breath, his gloved fingers tapping against the railing. His voice was calm, yet tinged with the unmistakable thrill of imminent conquest.

"They have no idea," Hoepner murmured.

Guderian did not look away from the horizon. His mind was already in motion, racing ahead to the logistics of Blitzkrieg, to the roads leading to Minsk and Smolensk, to the rivers that would have to be crossed, to the railways that would be seized and repurposed in the Reich's service.

He exhaled slowly.

"No," he answered at last. "They don't."

III. Soviet Unawareness
(Early May 1941 – Soviet Border Garrisons, Western Ukraine & Belarus)

The air over Brest-Litovsk was cool and still. The Red Army garrison near the border moved through its usual nightly routines, slow and unhurried.

From his post, Lieutenant Yuri Sokolov tapped his cigarette against the railing, the embers glowing briefly before fading. Across the river, German sentries moved in steady, deliberate patrols. They paced, stopped, exchanged a few words, then continued.

Same faces. Same movements. Same silence.

It had been like this for months.

Below, a few Soviet soldiers gathered. Their breath was visible in the crisp air. A flask passed between them, their laughter quiet and relaxed.

"Anything?" one of them asked, nodding toward the German side.

Sokolov took a slow drag from his cigarette, then shook his head.

"Nothing unusual. Same patrols."

His gaze shifted beyond the border, where watch lights shone through the trees. He had heard talk of German troop movements, of supply shipments increasing, of rail stations filling with munitions instead of grain. But the border remained quiet. The Germans—disciplined as always—gave no sign that war was near.

Behind him, a soldier stretched his arms and let out a tired sigh.

"Stalin was right," he muttered. "The Germans won't risk war with us."

Sokolov exhaled, watching the smoke disappear into the night sky.

IV. Final Meeting with Hitler
(May 14, 1941 – Führer Headquarters, Berlin)

The conference chamber of the Führer Headquarters was dimly lit, the only illumination coming from a single brass chandelier overhead and the glow of strategic lamps set upon the long wooden table. A tangible tension filled the air.

At the head of the table, Adolf Hitler stood motionless, his pale blue eyes gleaming with a sharp, unyielding intensity. He did not pace, did not fidget—he simply watched, his gaze moving slowly across the faces of the men before him.

They were the architects of war, gathered now for the final sanctioning of destruction.

Field Marshal Wilhelm Keitel sat with his usual rigid posture, a perfect portrait of obedience, his face unreadable but his agreement already given. To his left, General Alfred Jodl, Chief of Operations, kept his hands clasped, his mind already processing the details of the coming invasion. Next to him, General Franz Halder, the meticulous strategist, studied the vast map stretched across the table—a cartographic depiction of conquest that would soon become reality. Hermann Göring, Reichsmarschall of the Luftwaffe, lounged lazily in his chair, a smirk playing at his lips, his confidence in the German war machine unwavering.

Hitler finally spoke, his voice low, deliberate, absolute.

"The time has come."

Silence reigned.

CASCADING DIVERGENCE 1941 Lebensraum

He placed both hands on the table, his fingers splayed over the inked borders of the Soviet Union, as if he could crush it then and there.

"The Red Army will not withstand the fury of the Wehrmacht," Hitler continued. "It is a force held together by fear, weakened by incompetence, and led by a man who is too paranoid to see what is coming. We will strike them down in a matter of weeks."

His voice grew sharper, more forceful.

"Stalin is weak. His officers are incompetent. His people, disorganized. They will fall before us like rotten timber."

A murmur of approval rippled through the room. The words were spoken as prophecy, as certainty.

Yet not all in the room were so convinced.

Halder, ever the pragmatist, narrowed his gaze at the fine red arrows crisscrossing the map. Each one represented a thrust into Soviet territory, the planned movements of Army Group North, Center, and South. The strategy was flawless in design, but he knew that war rarely followed design.

He straightened slightly in his chair before speaking.

"Mein Führer," Halder said carefully, "if they do not collapse as expected—if their reserves run deeper than our intelligence suggests—we may require adjustments."

A thin silence followed.

Hitler's expression darkened slightly, his lips pressing together in irritation. Adjustments? There would be no adjustments.

"There will be no adjustments, General." His voice was clipped, firm. "This war will be won in months, not years."

Halder gave a curt nod, but exchanged a glance with von Brauchitsch, the Commander-in-Chief of the Army. The look was brief, but it spoke volumes.

Doubt.

Not spoken, never spoken, but there—lurking beneath the surface of their disciplined faces.

But doubt had no place here.

Hitler leaned forward, his hands pressing harder against the table, his presence looming over them all.

"Issue the final orders," he commanded.

His voice was absolute.

"We attack in eight days."

V. Eve of Destruction
(May 21, 1941 – The Last Night Before Barbarossa)

The moon hung low over the eastern horizon, a silver crescent above the forests and fields along the German-Soviet frontier. A thin mist drifted over the ground, curling between the dark shapes of Panzer divisions. Their steel hulls barely reflected the light.

There was no sound. No movement.

Thousands of German soldiers sat beside their vehicles, rifles cleaned, bayonets affixed. They waited. The entire front was a coiled spring, held tight, ready to snap.

CASCADING DIVERGENCE 1941 Lebensraum

At the forward positions of Army Group Center, a Panzer commander knelt beside his tank, adjusting the straps of his helmet. His eyes stayed on the barbed wire ahead, on the faint outline of Soviet watchtowers beyond no-man's land. The enemy was unaware. Unprepared. Soon, their world would be fire, smoke, and blood.

Farther back, at a Luftwaffe airbase in East Prussia, bomber crews gathered in the shadows of their Heinkel He 111 bombers. Dim floodlights cast long shadows across the tarmac. Some played cards. Others smoked, their cigarettes glowing in the dark. Some whispered. Others sat in silence.

They all knew what was coming.

Above them, the stars were still. Tomorrow, the sky would be filled with fire and smoke.

Inside OKH Headquarters, General Franz Halder stood alone in his office. He rubbed his temples, exhaustion pressing in. But his mind stayed sharp.

The plan was perfect. The Wehrmacht was in position. Everything was ready.

He took a slow breath, then opened his personal diary.

On the final page before the invasion, he wrote:

"Everything is in place. The greatest operation in military history begins tomorrow."

He closed the book.

Across the border, in a Soviet command post, a young Red Army officer leaned back in his chair, yawning. His uniform was wrinkled. His cap sat crooked. The night had been uneventful, like every night before.

A final glance at his paperwork. A signature here. A stamp there.

Then he stretched, arms raised.

Beyond the frontier, hidden in the forests, over three million German soldiers stood ready to storm his homeland.

6

The First Blows
May 22, 1941 – German-Soviet Borderlands

I. Last Moments of Peace

The eastern horizon had started to lighten, but dawn was still far off. A cold mist rolled over the empty fields beyond the Soviet border, clinging to the barbed wire fences.

Lieutenant Yuri Sokolov shifted his weight, adjusting the rifle strap on his shoulder as he stood in the wooden guard tower. His breath hung in the cold air, vanishing into the dark.

Below, a few Red Army sentries paced along the perimeter, their rifles slung lazily over their shoulders. Their movements were slow, almost bored. For months, they had watched the Germans drill, march, and shift positions—but never attack.

Across the border, German guards moved the same way, marching their usual patrols beneath the moonlight. Same routes, same shifts, same tired expressions. It had become a routine, almost an unspoken truce.

Sokolov exhaled, pulling his coat tighter. The Germans weren't going anywhere. Not tonight.

II. The Order to Attack

Deep inside a Wehrmacht command post, Field Marshal Fedor von Bock studied a map, tracing his finger over the planned advance. Thick black arrows stretched across the Soviet Union, driving straight toward Moscow.

The room was silent except for the hum of radio transmissions and the shuffle of boots. Officers waited for the final order.

Then, the field telephone rang. A sharp, clipped buzz.

An adjutant answered, listened, then turned to the room.

"Berlin has given the order. Operation Barbarossa begins at 04:15."

For a moment, no one moved.

Von Bock took a slow breath, then turned to General Franz Halder, his voice calm.

"Issue the final orders."

Halder straightened his uniform and gave a short nod.

"Codeword: Dortmund."

The radio operators moved quickly, hands turning dials, tapping keys. The message spread through hundreds of miles of communication lines, reaching command bunkers, field posts, and front-line trenches.

Engines rumbled to life. Soldiers gripped their rifles. Artillery crews loaded the first shells.

The war was about to begin.

CASCADING DIVERGENCE 1941 Lebensraum

III. Fire from the Sky

Major Ivan Gromyko woke to a low vibration in the ground. His cot rattled. A tin mug fell from the nightstand.

Then came the first explosion. A deep boom that shook the walls and sent dust drifting from the ceiling. A second blast followed. Then another.

The barracks windows shattered inward.

Gromyko was on his feet before he knew what was happening.

Sirens wailed.

Outside, pilots ran in every direction, some half-dressed, some shouting for orders that no one could give. The airfield searchlights swung wildly, catching glimpses of bombers overhead.

The next wave of explosions hit.

Soviet fighters parked in formation went up in flames as the bombs landed. Metal twisted, wings snapped, fuel tanks ignited. The concussive blasts sent men and debris flying.

Gromyko barely heard the shouts around him. He saw a young mechanic sprint toward an undamaged fighter, waving frantically—too late.

A bomb struck nearby, flipping the aircraft like a toy. The mechanic vanished in a fireball.

Some pilots made it to their planes, engines sputtering to life, but they never got off the ground.

Messerschmitts screamed overhead, strafing the runway. Machine-gun fire ripped through cockpits, shattered glass, ignited fuel lines. Pilots died before their planes could even move.

Gromyko ducked behind wreckage as another bomb tore through the tarmac.

Smoke filled the sky. The airfield was gone.

And in that moment, he knew—they had already lost the skies.

IV. The Border Shatters

The roar of the Luftwaffe still echoed in the distance. Smoke and flame rose into the night sky. But along the Soviet border, where thousands of Red Army soldiers stood at their posts, everything was silent.

Lieutenant Yuri Sokolov stood in his guard tower, gripping his rifle. His hands were still trembling from the distant explosions. Maybe it was nothing. Maybe it was just a border skirmish.

Then came the whistle.

A high-pitched shriek.

Sokolov barely had time to turn before the world exploded.

A wall of artillery fire rained down.

Howitzers. Mortars. Rocket launchers.

CASCADING DIVERGENCE 1941 Lebensraum

The ground convulsed beneath him as the first shells hit the Soviet border defenses. The wooden watchtower shook as a direct hit tore through its base.

It collapsed.

Sokolov fell with it.

He landed hard, the air knocked from his lungs. His ears rang. His vision blurred. Somewhere behind him, the barracks exploded—the entire building consumed in fire.

Through the dust and smoke, he saw them.

Figures, moving fast.

The Germans were already inside the wire.

The artillery barrage wasn't just an attack—it was the signal to advance.

Sokolov scrambled for his rifle. He could hear the distant rattle of machine guns, the clipped shouts of German officers giving orders.

Then came the first wave of MG-34 fire.

Men dropped where they stood. The Soviet line was already falling apart.

V. The Drive to Moscow Begins

A Wehrmacht command vehicle sped down a dirt road, the roar of its engine blending with distant artillery. Inside the command post, General Heinz Guderian sat at a steel-plated table, radio transmissions pouring in.

His officers relayed updates. The attack had begun barely 45 minutes ago, but already, the Wehrmacht's Panzer divisions were breaking through.

A staff officer approached with a newly decoded communiqué. He placed it on the table.

"From Army Group Center, Herr General."

Guderian scanned the message, then smiled.

Brest-Litovsk defenses collapsing. Forward elements securing the city.

Luftwaffe confirms air superiority. Soviet response negligible.

Panzer formations advancing toward Minsk. No significant resistance.

One of his officers hesitated. "We expected more of a fight at the river crossings."

Guderian leaned back, satisfied. He had spent years refining Blitzkrieg. But even he hadn't expected this level of collapse.

"They weren't ready," he said simply. "They never believed we would come."

He turned to his operations chief.

"At this rate," he muttered, more to himself than anyone, "we'll be in Moscow by August."

Silence filled the room.

If true, this would be unthinkable—the Soviet capital, Stalin's stronghold, captured in mere months.

CASCADING DIVERGENCE 1941 Lebensraum

One officer finally spoke. "If they don't rally their forces."

Guderian snorted.

"They won't."

Outside, columns of German tanks surged forward, their tracks grinding over Soviet soil. Overhead, Messerschmitt fighters streaked across the sky, clearing the way.

The war had begun.

And Germany was already winning.

RON WOOD

CASCADING DIVERGENCE 1941 Lebensraum

7

Red Army in Chaos
May 22–24, 1941 – Soviet Western Fronts, Belarus & Ukraine

I. Kremlin in Crisis
(May 22, 1941 – 05:30 Hours, Moscow, Kremlin)

The red telephone rang. Its sharp, metallic tone echoed through the dimly lit office. The air was heavy.

Josef Stalin sat motionless behind his desk, fingers drumming slowly against the polished wood. Scattered intelligence reports lay before him—unread, ignored. He had skimmed them once. Nothing had seemed urgent.

But the phone kept ringing.

Across from him, Molotov sat in silence, his shoulders stiff beneath his well-worn coat. General Georgy Zhukov, Chief of the General Staff, stood with his arms crossed, his jaw tight, his eyes fixed on the door. In the corner, Beria paced like a predator in a cage, muttering darkly under his breath.

Three rings. Four. Five.

Still, Stalin didn't move.

Zhukov exchanged a glance with Molotov. "It may be from the front," he said cautiously.

At last, Stalin reached forward and lifted the receiver with a slow, deliberate motion.

"This is Stalin," he said.

Static crackled. Then a voice—Timoshenko's—came through. Clear. Urgent. Background noise filtered in—raised voices, muffled shouting, distant gunfire, radios buzzing with chaos.

"Comrade Stalin. We are under attack."

Zhukov's eyes snapped toward the phone.

"Where?" Stalin asked, his voice still steady, but with a faint edge.

"Everywhere," Timoshenko replied. "The Germans crossed the border just after first light. They're bombing our airfields, advancing on multiple fronts. Brest-Litovsk is surrounded. Our western lines are breaking."

A pause. Stalin's hand tightened around the phone.

"This cannot be correct," he said, the words slow, like a man refusing to step off a cliff. "There has been no declaration."

Timoshenko's voice sharpened. "This isn't a diplomatic maneuver, Comrade Stalin. This is war. I'm calling from the Western Command post—our outer defenses are being overrun. The Luftwaffe is targeting every known airfield. Minsk and Kiev will be next. We need authorization to mobilize reserves now or we will have no line left to defend."

CASCADING DIVERGENCE 1941 Lebensraum

Silence.

Zhukov stepped forward. "The reports we've received are consistent. Every hour we delay—"

Stalin raised a hand, silencing him.

"Hold your positions until further instructions," Stalin said flatly into the phone.

"But—"

Stalin hung up.

The room was dead silent.

Zhukov clenched his jaw. His voice, when he spoke, trembled with barely contained fury.

"He still doesn't believe it," he muttered.

Molotov removed his glasses and rubbed his eyes.

"He will," he said quietly.

Beyond the Kremlin's thick walls, Berlin's trap was already closing.

II. Disaster Unfolds
(May 22–23, 1941 – Soviet Western Fronts, Belarus & Ukraine)

The sun had barely risen over Belarus, casting long shadows over the fields. For the Red Army, the night had never ended.

The German Blitzkrieg was not just an attack—it was a storm. A tidal wave of destruction tearing through the Soviet frontier at impossible speed.

In Belarus, the 3rd and 10th Soviet Armies were surrounded within hours. Entire divisions, still waiting for orders, lost communication. Their radios went silent. Commanders shouted into dead receivers, desperate for guidance. None came. The Wehrmacht was already upon them.

At Brest-Litovsk, the fortress garrison fought with fanatical resistance. They retreated into bunkers and tunnels, turning each courtyard into a battlefield. But Wehrmacht artillery did not stop. Stone walls crumbled under relentless shelling.

Inside a bunker, a young Soviet lieutenant, his uniform stained with blood and soot, clutched his rifle. Dust and fire choked the air. Explosions shook the ground. His men screamed. Some fought. Others cried out in pain. Outside, the Germans advanced—inch by inch, bunker by bunker, trench by trench.

By nightfall on May 22nd, the fortress was a tomb. The last defenders fell. The Red Flag was torn down, replaced by the black cross of the Wehrmacht.

But Brest-Litovsk was only the beginning.

Western Ukraine—Total Collapse

The situation was worse.

Soviet tank divisions, the backbone of the defense, were thrown into chaotic counterattacks. No coordination. No air support. No strategy.

What followed was a massacre.

German Panzers, precise and disciplined, moved like hunters. They flanked Soviet tanks, striking from multiple directions. Before the Soviets could react, they were already being torn apart.

The Luftwaffe ruled the skies. Stukas and Messerschmitts stalked convoys, their bombs turning Soviet supply lines into flaming wrecks.

A Soviet T-26 tank, its paint still fresh, rolled forward. The commander shouted orders, his head barely visible from the hatch.

Then, the scream of a Stuka siren.

The ground erupted.

The blast lifted the tank off its treads, flipping it onto its side like a child's toy. The commander never had time to scream.

Highways of Desperation

The roads east became a flood of broken men.

Thousands of Soviet soldiers, tank crews, and civilians poured onto the highways, fleeing in every direction. Some ran. Some dropped their rifles. Some just stared, blank-faced, their spirits broken.

The scale of the disaster was too much to comprehend.

III. Stalin's Seclusion
(May 23, 1941 – 03:00 Hours, Kremlin, Moscow)

The Kremlin was silent.

Not the usual kind of silence, where a ticking clock or the distant echo of footsteps filled the void. No, this was a hollow, dreadful silence, the kind that settles over a city before a storm, before something irreversible happens.

The Soviet government had been paralyzed.

Josef Stalin, the man who had ruled the USSR with absolute authority, had simply vanished.

He had left the Kremlin late that night, slipping away without a word, retreating to his dacha outside Moscow. No one had seen him since. No new orders had come. The Soviet Union, under its strongest ruler, had been left without a leader in its darkest hour.

Inside the Kremlin, in Stalin's now-abandoned office, a small group of men sat in silence.

Zhukov. Timoshenko. Molotov. Beria.

They were the highest-ranking officials of the Soviet Union, but in that moment, they were nothing more than men sitting in a burning house, waiting for someone to tell them what to do.

No one spoke.

Finally, General Georgy Zhukov—the man upon whom the future of the Red Army now rested—broke the silence.

"This is a catastrophe."

His words carried no emotion, just cold, blunt truth.

Across the table, Molotov adjusted his glasses, his voice measured but distant. "He will return."

Zhukov's jaw clenched.

CASCADING DIVERGENCE 1941 Lebensraum

"And until then?" He turned to face them, his patience wearing thin. "We let the Germans march to Moscow?"

Beria, leaning back in his chair, tapped his fingers rhythmically against the wooden armrest. He smiled slightly, but it wasn't a warm smile—it was the sneer of a man who enjoyed watching others squirm.

"We will act," he said smoothly, his voice dripping with something unreadable, "when Stalin tells us to act."

Zhukov had heard enough.

He shot to his feet, his palms slamming onto the desk, his uniform disheveled from lack of sleep.

"We need to mobilize now!"

Molotov, ever calm, ever the politician, met Zhukov's gaze without flinching.

"Then do it."

A beat passed.

Zhukov held his breath, waiting for someone—anyone—to challenge him. To argue.

No one did.

Without waiting for further discussion, Zhukov turned on his heel and strode out of the office.

He would give the orders himself—with or without Stalin's approval.

IV. Domination by the Luftwaffe
(May 23, 1941 – Soviet Airfields, Belarus & Ukraine)

The sky belonged to Germany.

From the moment the first bombs fell, the Luftwaffe had seized total control, striking with merciless precision. The Red Air Force, caught flat-footed, had suffered the worst disaster in its history.

At the few surviving air bases that hadn't been obliterated in the opening strike, chaos reigned.

At a bomb-scarred Soviet airfield near Minsk, a group of mechanics and ground crew scrambled frantically, trying to refuel a cluster of MiG-3 fighters still miraculously intact. Smoke curled from burning wreckage, the ruins of what had once been a fleet of over a hundred Soviet aircraft.

A pilot, his uniform soaked in sweat, vaulted into his cockpit, yanking his oxygen mask into place.

"Clear the runway!" a crew chief screamed.

The MiG-3's engine roared to life, coughing black smoke as the fighter lurched forward, its tires kicking up clouds of dust and ash.

No sooner had he started his ascent when the whine of approaching engines filled the air.

The Soviet pilot barely had time to react before a formation of Messerschmitt Bf 109s swooped down like hawks.

The first burst of machine-gun fire ripped through his wing, sending his aircraft into a violent spiral. He fought the stick,

CASCADING DIVERGENCE 1941 Lebensraum

trying to level out, but another cannon round struck his fuselage, the cockpit exploding into a ball of flame.

The German fighter planes never even broke formation.

They made pass after pass, machine guns raking the runway, setting fuel trucks and ammunition depots ablaze. Hangars collapsed, consumed by roaring infernos, while Soviet aircrews died where they stood, cut down before they could even fire a shot.

A lone Soviet anti-aircraft gun—one of the few still intact—opened fire from a sandbagged position near the perimeter.

For a brief moment, a Messerschmitt wobbled, smoke trailing from its wingtip.

It wasn't enough.

A German Stuka banked sharply, its siren screaming as it dove, releasing a single, deadly payload.

The bunker disappeared in an instant, a fireball of debris and shattered bodies.

By midday on May 23, the last remnants of the Soviet air force were gone.

The few pilots who managed to take off found themselves outnumbered, outgunned, and overmatched.

The iconic red stars on their aircraft made them easy prey for the Luftwaffe's experienced fighter aces. The Soviet I-16s and MiG-3s, fast but lightly armored, were ripped apart in the air, their burning wreckage spiraling down to the forests and fields below.

On the ground, commanders at Soviet air bases sent desperate radio calls to Moscow, pleading for orders, reinforcements, anything.

There was no response.

The German bombers now had free rein, striking supply lines, railways, bridges, and retreating Red Army convoys without resistance.

A column of Soviet trucks, fleeing eastward, wound through a narrow dirt road, their tires kicking up thick clouds of dust. Inside one of them, a young conscript clutched his rifle, his hands trembling as he peered through the canvas flaps at the sky above.

Then came the shadows.

The Stukas appeared first, emerging from the clouds like ghosts of death, their engines howling, their wings adorned with the unmistakable black cross of the Reich.

By the time the Soviets realized what was happening, it was too late.

The first bombs hit dead center, turning the front of the convoy into a smoldering ruin.

More explosions followed, trucks flipping into the air like matchsticks, men thrown from the wreckage, their screams swallowed by the roar of fire.

A Soviet officer crawled from the burning wreckage of his transport, coughing, his uniform stained with soot and blood. He looked up, dazed, as a lone Messerschmitt streaked past, its wings gleaming in the sunlight.

CASCADING DIVERGENCE 1941 Lebensraum

It looped back.

The German pilot lined up his shot, and a second later, the officer was gone.

By the time the second day of war had ended, the Luftwaffe had done the impossible.

The entire Soviet Western Front was blind.

With no air support, no reconnaissance, no coordination, the Red Army was now fighting in darkness, while the Germans moved with deadly precision.

V. Germans Race Forward
(May 24, 1941 – Wehrmacht Forward Command, Near Smolensk)

The map before him told the story.

Red lines, meant to mark the Soviet defensive positions, were already irrelevant.

Army Group Center's Panzers had smashed through them all, and now, the Wehrmacht was racing eastward, moving faster than any campaign in military history.

General Heinz Guderian stood over the command table, scanning the latest intelligence reports as fresh communiqués from his advancing divisions flooded in.

A staff officer, still breathless from his dash into the war room, saluted and began reading.

"General, Army Group Center has advanced more than 150 kilometers in two days. Minimal Soviet resistance remains intact. The 3rd and 10th Soviet Armies are in full retreat."

Guderian barely reacted. He had expected a fight—perhaps even a grueling battle of attrition.

Instead, he had found a broken enemy.

The Soviets were not just losing ground; they were collapsing in real time.

At this rate, Smolensk was only days away.

The clatter of boots announced the arrival of a junior officer, a message from Berlin clutched tightly in his gloved hands.

He handed it over.

Guderian scanned the message in silence, his expression unreadable, before finally setting it down on the table.

"High Command is urging continued rapid movement. The destruction of the Red Army remains the priority."

A chuckle rippled through the room.

One of the officers sneered.

"At this rate, we'll be in Smolensk within days."

Guderian lifted his gaze, locking eyes with his men.

His smile was razor-sharp.

"Then let's not keep them waiting."

He turned to the radio operators.

"Signal all divisions: No delays. No waiting for reinforcements. We press forward. Tonight, we camp closer to Moscow."

CASCADING DIVERGENCE 1941 Lebensraum

Outside, the growl of engines filled the air as armored columns roared to life, tank treads grinding over the dirt roads, kicking up thick clouds of dust.

They moved as a single unstoppable force, plunging deeper into the heart of Russia, devouring territory by the hour.

RON WOOD

8

Soviet Counterattack
May 24–27, 1941 – Soviet Western Fronts, Belarus & Ukraine

I. Red Army Decides to Strike Back
(May 24, 1941 – Soviet Headquarters, Moscow)

The Kremlin war room was thick with smoke, sweat, and failure.

The stench of stale tobacco clung to the air, mingling with the damp ink of battle maps that lay scattered across the long wooden table, their surfaces defiled by frantic scrawls and blood-red notations.

The weight of disaster pressed down on the men inside.

Marshal Semyon Timoshenko, the People's Commissar for Defense, leaned heavily on the table, his uniform rumpled, his collar unbuttoned, as though loosening the fabric might somehow loosen the noose tightening around the Soviet Union.

His eyes were bloodshot, his body exhausted, but there was no time for rest.

Across from him, General Georgy Zhukov, the newly appointed Chief of the General Staff, silently flipped through the latest intelligence reports, his fingers tense against the brittle pages.

The silence was unbearable.

Then, Zhukov muttered, his voice hollow, as if saying the words made them real:

"The Germans are beyond Minsk."

Timoshenko's fingers curled into a fist against the table.

"We have to counterattack immediately."

Zhukov's head snapped up. Anger flickered in his eyes.

"Counterattack?" he said, almost in disbelief.

The Red Army was in no position to attack anything.

The front was collapsing. Their divisions were scattered, their supply lines in tatters, and the Luftwaffe dominated the skies. Soviet commanders had no clear picture of the battle—German Panzers were moving too fast, cutting through Soviet formations like scythes through wheat.

Yet Timoshenko was right about one thing.

If they did nothing, the Germans would be in Smolensk within days.

"Where do we strike?" Zhukov asked, forcing himself to think like a strategist, not a man watching his army disintegrate.

CASCADING DIVERGENCE 1941 Lebensraum

Timoshenko's finger stabbed down at the map, just west of Minsk.

"Here. The 5th and 6th Mechanized Corps. If we hit the Germans here, we can slow their advance—buy time to regroup."

Zhukov's jaw tightened.

The 5th and 6th Mechanized Corps were among the best-equipped units left, their armor divisions still relatively intact. But they had already suffered losses in the chaotic opening days of the invasion.

Their fuel was running dangerously low. Their ammunition reserves were dwindling.

And worst of all, they would be going up against Germany's best.

Heinz Guderian, Hermann Hoth, Erwin Rommel.

Men who had rewritten the art of armored warfare.

Zhukov's hands clenched into white-knuckled fists.

He had no illusions about what this meant. The Red Army was fighting blindly, its commanders scrambling to improvise against an enemy that had been preparing for months.

And yet—what choice did they have?

He inhaled deeply, feeling the weight of the moment settle over him.

"Do it."

The order was given.

The Red Army would strike back.

And God help them all.

II. Rommel's Report
(May 24, 1941 – Wehrmacht Forward Command, Near Minsk)

Rommel stood atop his command half-track, dust swirling around him as his Panzers pushed forward, engines roaring like a storm rolling across the steppe. He lowered his binoculars, eyes fixed on the horizon where Soviet armor had begun to mass. Finally, they were making their move. Without turning, he extended a hand. An aide immediately grabbed a field notebook, flipping to a fresh page and readying his pen.

"Take this down," Rommel said, his voice steady despite the battlefield chaos around him. "To the commander of Army Group Center. Situation report—Eastern Advance."

The aide's pen scratched across the paper as Rommel dictated, his words quick and precise. He spoke as he always did—without hesitation, without uncertainty. His orders were clear, his confidence absolute. The Soviets thought they could halt him here, but they had underestimated him. They always did.

When Rommel finished, his aide snapped the notebook shut. "Transmit that immediately," Rommel ordered, already stepping off the half-track. "Then tell the officers to be ready. We're moving."

CASCADING DIVERGENCE 1941 Lebensraum

As the radio operator rushed to send the message, Rommel pulled his gloves tighter, his gaze fixed eastward. The battle was coming, and he was already thinking three steps ahead.

To: Commander, Army Group Center

From: General Erwin Rommel

Subject: Situation Report – Eastern Advance

Herr General,

The advance east of Minsk is proceeding faster than anticipated. Our Panzer columns are maintaining formation, and despite the rough terrain, the momentum remains with us. The roads are little more than dust and wreckage, but that has not slowed us. Oil, smoke, and fire mark our path forward.

Enemy resistance has been scattered. We have encountered burned-out convoys and hastily abandoned positions, but little in the way of a coordinated defense. If this continues, we will be across the Berezina sooner than planned.

However, the Soviets are finally stirring. My reconnaissance units report enemy armor moving toward our right flank. It appears they have chosen this moment to make their stand.

Good. We will meet them head-on. My Panzers are already adjusting their formations. My officers know what to do. We will not lose momentum.

The Soviets may believe they have the advantage, but we will remind them why we move faster than anyone else. Speed wins battles. I expect full control of this sector by nightfall. Will send further updates once the enemy has been dealt with.

Rommel

III. Soviet Counterattack Collapses
(May 25, 1941 – Near Borisov, Belarus)

The ground trembled beneath the weight of Soviet armor.

Columns of T-26 and BT-7 tanks, their turrets bobbing over the uneven terrain, churned up clouds of dust, the roar of diesel engines deafening over the low hum of battlefield tension. The 5th and 6th Mechanized Corps had been given their orders—strike Rommel's overextended flank, crush his momentum, and stall the German advance toward Minsk.

At the head of the charge, Colonel Mikhail Katukov sat rigidly in his command vehicle, his knuckles white against the radio receiver.

"Hold formation!" he barked into the static-laced frequency.

His men had drilled for this moment. But this was not an exercise.

The stakes were clear—if they failed here, the fall of Minsk would be a certainty.

Katukov's jaw clenched. He was no fool—he knew the odds were against them.

The Luftwaffe still ruled the skies, German anti-tank guns were vastly superior, and worse—they were attacking blindly. Soviet reconnaissance had been limited, erratic, incomplete. They had no clear picture of what lay ahead.

But orders were orders.

Then—the world around them exploded into fire.

Rommel had been waiting for them.

CASCADING DIVERGENCE 1941 Lebensraum

The first shots came from the tree line ahead, where camouflaged German 88mm anti-tank guns lay in perfect concealment.

The first row of Soviet tanks never had a chance.

The sharp crack of high-velocity shells echoed across the battlefield, and in an instant, flaming wreckage replaced what had once been an armored spearhead.

A T-26 took a direct hit to its turret, the explosion sending its hatch spiraling into the air like a severed limb. The crew never escaped—fire consumed them before they could even scream.

Another shell punched through the hull of a BT-7, igniting its fuel reserves. The tank detonated in a fiery burst, the shockwave hurling nearby infantry to the ground.

Katukov barely had time to process the devastation before Rommel's second hammer blow landed.

From the hills beyond, German Panzer IVs surged forward, their guns barking with precision, slicing through Soviet formations like a blade through flesh.

Rommel's half-tracks charged alongside them, their machine guns raking through Soviet infantry, bodies falling like cut wheat under the relentless hail of bullets.

And then—the sky howled.

The Stukas arrived, their screaming sirens wailing like mechanical banshees, their shadows sliding like reapers over the battlefield below.

The first bombs fell.

A direct hit obliterated an entire column of advancing Soviet armor, sending burning husks tumbling across the field like discarded toys.

Another split a Soviet artillery position in half, the gun crews incinerated before they could even load a shell.

Katukov's radio was now a chaos of frantic voices, screaming, crying, and static.

"We're being flanked!"

"Where is our air support?! We need air support—NOW!"

"Tanks are burning—God help us!"

The sky answered only with the shriek of another Stuka dive.

Katukov never saw the shell that hit him.

A high-explosive round slammed into his command vehicle, flipping it onto its side with brutal force.

His head snapped back, colliding with the cold steel interior.

The world around him spun, darkened, faded.

Within one hour, the entire Soviet counterattack had disintegrated.

The once mighty armored assault was nothing more than a scattering of burning tanks, shattered bodies, and desperate men fleeing eastward.

By nightfall, the battlefield was silent except for the crackle of flames licking at ruined war machines.

CASCADING DIVERGENCE 1941 Lebensraum

Rommel stood atop his tank, his boots coated in dust and victory, watching as hundreds of Soviet prisoners were marched past him.

Their hands raised, their eyes hollow with defeat, they shuffled forward, past the wreckage of their failed counterattack.

This was not a battle—it was a slaughter.

IV. Aftermath
(May 26, 1941 – Wehrmacht Forward Command, Near Smolensk)

Inside Wehrmacht headquarters were the lingering remnants of a long night spent pouring over battle maps and casualty reports. At the center of it all, Field Marshal Fedor von Bock stood motionless, his sharp eyes scanning the latest intelligence dispatches laid out before him. He already knew what they would say—the Soviet counterattack had been crushed before it had ever truly begun.

The previous day, Rommel had lured the Soviets into an ambush, annihilating their armor and sending their forces into a full-scale rout. There had been no follow-up attacks, no desperate reorganization of Soviet lines, nothing to suggest they had any remaining strategic capability to stall the advance. The Red Army, at least in this sector, had ceased to function as a coherent fighting force.

A courier stepped forward, placing another communiqué onto the desk. Von Bock reached for it absently, his fingers brushing over the crisp folds of the message before unfolding it.

It was from Rommel.

Soviet resistance collapsing. Request permission to advance beyond Smolensk immediately.

Von Bock exhaled slowly, rubbing his chin.

Rommel was always pushing forward, always hungry for more ground, always impatient with the constraints of operational planning. It was that recklessness that made him both the Wehrmacht's greatest asset and its most unpredictable force.

By doctrine, the army was supposed to pause, consolidate, secure logistics before moving further—but von Bock knew Rommel would ignore such restrictions if they were imposed. If he had his way, he would be rolling into Moscow before the first snows of autumn.

Von Bock weighed his options.

He should tell Rommel to slow down, to wait for the main infantry divisions to catch up, to ensure his supply lines weren't overextended.

Instead, he looked up, nodding toward his radio officer.

"Send him a message."

The radio operator adjusted his headset, waiting.

Von Bock paused for only a second before speaking.

"Keep going."

V. Last Hope of the Red Army
(May 27, 1941 – Kremlin, Moscow)

The air inside Stalin's office was stale, unmoving, thick with the oppressive weight of failure and fear. The walls, once lined with portraits of Lenin and banners of Soviet strength, now seemed to close in, trapping those inside in a world rapidly crumbling beneath them. The muffled sounds of the city outside—car horns, distant footsteps—felt surreal, disconnected from the disaster that was unfolding beyond the Kremlin walls.

Josef Stalin sat behind his desk, his broad shoulders hunched slightly forward, his fingers steepled beneath his chin. His usually unyielding gaze was sunken, his face drawn, lined with the weight of news that only a day ago he would have called impossible. Yet his voice, when he spoke, remained like iron.

"Report."

The room was deathly silent before General Georgy Zhukov finally cleared his throat. The Chief of the General Staff, always a disciplined and calculating soldier, spoke with careful precision, though his voice carried a rare, bitter edge.

"Comrade Stalin, our counterattack has failed."

Stalin's fingers twitched, but he remained still.

"The Germans have broken through our defenses at multiple points. Minsk will fall within days." Zhukov hesitated, then continued, choosing his words carefully. "Army Group Center is advancing at speeds beyond our projections. We no longer have sufficient forces to slow them before Smolensk."

Stalin exhaled slowly, his eyes shifting toward Timoshenko. The older man, his uniform disheveled, his face slick with sweat, nodded grimly. Everything Zhukov had said was true.

For the first time, a terrible realization settled into Stalin's mind—a thought he had dismissed for weeks, crushed under his own certainty that Hitler would never dare such foolishness.

Now, the reality loomed before him like a steel blade pressed against his throat.

"Then we will form a new line," Stalin said at last. His voice was measured, slow, but the men in the room could hear the effort it took to keep it steady.

He leaned back in his chair, lighting a fresh pipe, the glow of embers flickering in the dim room. The smoke curled upward, twisting like the threads of fate that had slipped from his grasp.

"We will defend Smolensk. We will not let them reach Moscow."

Zhukov did not respond immediately. Instead, he watched Stalin closely, searching his expression, reading the unspoken words beneath the surface.

Because they both knew the truth.

The Germans were moving faster than anyone had imagined—and the Red Army was running out of time.

CASCADING DIVERGENCE 1941 Lebensraum

9

Road to Smolensk

May 27–June 10, 1941 – Soviet Western Front, Belarus & Ukraine

I. Unstoppable Drive of Army Group Center

(May 27, 1941 – Wehrmacht Forward Command, Near Borisov, Belarus)

The countryside east of Minsk was a landscape of ruin, a scarred battlefield marked by fire and destruction. The roads, once sturdy pathways through the Belarusian plains, were now clogged with wreckage—burnt-out Soviet trucks twisted into smoldering skeletons, overturned supply wagons, and the bodies of soldiers who never had a chance to retreat.

German Panzer divisions surged forward, their formations tight, disciplined, relentless. They moved like an unstoppable tide, steel and fury crashing upon the shattered remnants of the Soviet forces. What little resistance remained was swept aside as columns of armor and mechanized infantry pressed forward, devouring the landscape mile by mile.

General Erwin Rommel, perched atop the turret of his command tank, surveyed the battlefield through his binoculars. His face was impassive, but his keen eyes took in every detail—the smoldering remains of Soviet anti-tank positions, the scattered Soviet soldiers fleeing into the forests, the occasional desperate attempt by Red Army officers to rally their men into one last stand—a stand that never lasted long against the onslaught of Blitzkrieg.

His Panzer Corps had obliterated the last semblance of order among the Soviet divisions near Borisov. Two hundred kilometers in five days.

That was how far they had advanced—a staggering speed, even by the lightning-fast standards of the Wehrmacht. In France, it had taken weeks to reach such distances. Here, in the vast, exposed plains of Russia, the advance was even swifter.

A staff officer approached, boots kicking up dust as he climbed onto the side of the tank, dispatch in hand.

"Herr General," the officer reported, "Army High Command confirms Soviet reinforcements massing near Smolensk."

Rommel lowered the binoculars, allowing himself a small, knowing smirk.

"They won't get there in time."

He knew it. Everyone knew it. The Soviets were collapsing too quickly, their formations breaking down before they could regroup. With the counterattack crushed days earlier, the road to Smolensk lay wide open.

And Smolensk was key.

CASCADING DIVERGENCE 1941 Lebensraum

If they took the city quickly, the entire Soviet Western Front would disintegrate. There would be nothing left between the Wehrmacht and Moscow itself.

In the distance, dark plumes of smoke twisted into the sky—Soviet supply depots burning, munitions caches exploding, entire columns of Red Army vehicles reduced to charred husks. The Luftwaffe dominated the skies, ensuring that no Soviet retreat could be organized, no reserves could be resupplied.

This was not just an advance—it was an annihilation.

Rommel turned to his radio operator, voice crisp, decisive.

"Signal all units. No delays. We keep moving."

II. Struggle of the Soviet High Command
(May 28, 1941 – Kremlin, Moscow)

The Kremlin war room was unusually cold. No one spoke. A half-finished cup of tea sat untouched, a thin film forming over its surface—a testament to how long they had been sitting in silence.

At the head of the table, Josef Stalin stood motionless, his deep-set eyes fixed on the map. His expression was unreadable, but his fingers—tapping, steady, deliberate—betrayed his thoughts.

His empire was bleeding away before him.

Marshal Semyon Timoshenko, his uniform disheveled, his eyes sunken from days without sleep, leaned forward, his hand pressing against Smolensk on the map. His voice was urgent, but controlled.

"Comrade Stalin, we must hold this city at all costs. If we lose Smolensk, we lose the gateway to Moscow."

The words hung in the air, but Stalin remained silent.

From across the room, General Georgy Zhukov folded his arms, his expression grim. He had already given the order to reinforce Smolensk, but he knew the truth. The reinforcements were few, their supply lines strained, their equipment already burning in the fields of Belarus.

Stalin's eyes turned toward him. "What about reinforcements from the south?"

Timoshenko hesitated. His lips parted slightly, but the answer was already written across his weary face.

"There are none."

Silence.

The only sound in the room was the soft tick of a wall clock.

Zhukov exhaled slowly.

"The Germans are moving faster than we can respond," he admitted. His voice was calm, but there was a note of finality in it, an unspoken acknowledgment of the impending disaster.

"We need time to form a new defensive line."

Stalin's jaw tightened, his fingers curling into a fist.

"Time," he muttered, his voice barely above a whisper. "Time is something we do not have."

CASCADING DIVERGENCE 1941 Lebensraum

III. Army Group North's Push to Leningrad
(May 29–June 5, 1941 – Baltic Front, Latvia & Estonia)

German Panzer formations thundered through the Baltic states, their iron hulls streaked with soot. Unstoppable. Unrelenting. They were hungry for Leningrad.

The Blitzkrieg had reached Estonia.

In Latvia, Field Marshal Wilhelm von Leeb stood in his makeshift headquarters, studying the grimy battle maps before him. His fingers traced the roads leading to his prize.

Behind him, an officer adjusted radio frequencies, waiting for the latest reports.

The news was better than expected.

"Riga has fallen," an adjutant reported, handing von Leeb a communiqué. "The Soviets barely fought. Our troops are already in Estonia. The Red Army is retreating toward Leningrad—but many are being cut off before they can escape."

Von Leeb nodded. For a moment, his stoic expression cracked—a moment of satisfaction.

"Excellent. If we press hard, they'll never regroup in time."

His officers exchanged glances. Their advance was surpassing all projections.

The Soviets were too slow. Their armies too scattered. Their logistics a disaster.

Army Group Center had ripped through Belarus, severing Soviet supply lines, stranding entire units in the Baltics.

This was how an empire crumbled—

Not in glorious last stands, but in disorderly retreats.

Not in heroic charges, but in frantic radio calls.

Not in bold commands, but in panicked Soviet officers realizing their armies were disappearing.

Von Leeb exhaled slowly. A small, measured victory.

"We will reach Leningrad before summer ends."

His voice was calm. Certain.

Leningrad was not ready.

Its defenses were weak. The Soviets never believed Germany would strike this soon.

They were wrong.

IV. Army Group South's Battle for Ukraine
(June 1–5, 1941 – Ukraine Front)

The heat in the south was nothing like the cool, crisp advance of Rommel's armored ghosts in Belarus or von Leeb's unchallenged march toward Leningrad. Here, in Ukraine, the Red Army was dug in, bloodied but fighting with teeth bared. The battle was not a sprint but a grinding war of attrition, and for the first time in this campaign, the Germans found themselves pushing against resistance that refused to break.

Field Marshal Gerd von Rundstedt, commander of Army Group South, stood beneath a tattered canopy at his forward command post near Lvov, eyes fixed on the maps pinned to the wall before him. The thick, smudged red lines, drawn hastily by his intelligence officers, marked the Soviet defensive positions—lines that, despite two days of constant attack, had not yet collapsed.

A staff officer entered, stiff-backed, saluting crisply.

"Report." Von Rundstedt didn't look up from the map.

"Soviets still holding defensive positions near Kiev, Herr Feldmarschall," the officer relayed. His voice lacked the usual certainty.

Von Rundstedt let out a slow exhale, his expression betraying no emotion, but inwardly, he felt a rare frustration. Kiev had not fallen in hours, as expected. Kharkov still stood. Unlike the shattered Soviet formations in Belarus, the Red Army in Ukraine was dug in like a cornered wolf, refusing to collapse.

The difference was clear—Ukraine was an industrial heartland, a region of vital factories, railways, and farmland. Its commanders knew they could not afford to lose it, and so they were throwing everything they had into delaying the inevitable. They weren't trying to win—they were trying to stall.

Von Rundstedt turned from the map and motioned to his radio operators.

"Send word to von Kleist. Tell him to break their river defenses before nightfall. We cannot waste time here."

General Ewald von Kleist, the ruthless Panzer leader driving toward Kiev, had so far encountered fierce opposition at the

Dnieper crossings. The Soviets had fortified the bridges and were fighting street by street to slow the German advance.

But von Rundstedt knew the truth behind the struggle.

Ukraine didn't have to fall quickly.

It just had to hold long enough to keep Soviet reinforcements from going north.

His orders were clear—lock the Red Army in battle here, keep them fighting, keep them bleeding, keep them desperate. Because every Soviet unit tied up in Ukraine was one less unit defending Moscow.

And if Army Group Center took Smolensk, it wouldn't matter how long Kiev held.

Because by then, Germany would be at Moscow's doorstep.

V. Race for Smolensk
(June 6–10, 1941 – Near Smolensk, Soviet Western Front)

The roar of tank engines filled the morning air, their rumble blending with the distant echoes of Soviet artillery fire. Rommel's Panzer Corps had arrived at Smolensk.

But this time, the Soviets were waiting.

Inside the turret of his command tank, Rommel raised his binoculars, scanning the horizon beyond the wheat fields. Unlike in Minsk, where Soviet resistance had shattered like glass, the defenders of Smolensk had been given time to dig in—and they had used it well.

Long trench networks ran parallel to the main roads, lined with anti-tank guns that glistened in the sun, their barrels aimed directly at the German advance. Soviet artillery held the high ground, its guns camouflaged along the rolling hills, waiting for the Wehrmacht's first push.

Most concerning, however, were the Soviet T-34s.

Rommel watched as a formation of the heavy, sloped-armored beasts rolled into position, dust kicking up in their wake. He had read reports about them, but seeing them in the field was another matter entirely. The T-34 was faster than any Soviet tank he had faced before—and worse, its cannon could penetrate the armor of his Panzers at a range that outmatched the German 37mm shells.

"This," Rommel muttered, "is going to be a real fight."

A radio operator climbed up to the hatch of Rommel's tank, his expression uneasy.

"Herr General, orders from Field Marshal von Bock. He wants us to wait for infantry reinforcements before engaging."

Rommel lowered his binoculars. His expression did not change.

"No."

The young officer hesitated. "Sir?"

"If we wait, they will reinforce further," Rommel explained, his voice calm, absolute. "We strike now."

He turned to his tank commanders, his steel-blue eyes alive with a predator's instinct.

"Full attack."

A pause.

"We take Smolensk today."

Within moments, the battle began.

A flurry of radio orders crackled across German frequencies, and the first wave of Panzers roared forward, their guns already blazing. Tracer rounds streaked the sky, cutting through the smoke as the Wehrmacht surged toward the Soviet defenses.

From the trenches, Soviet anti-tank crews scrambled into position, their 76mm guns belching fire. A Panzer III at the front of the charge erupted in flames, its hatch flying open as the crew inside was incinerated.

Rommel's jaw tightened.

This was not Minsk.

This was Smolensk—and here, the Red Army had come to fight.

10

Fall of Smolensk

June 10–20, 1941 – Soviet Western Front, Smolensk, USSR

I. The Battle Begins
(June 10, 1941 – Outskirts of Smolensk, Soviet Western Front)

The fields outside Smolensk trembled under the relentless barrage of artillery fire. Shells screamed overhead, their detonations sending shockwaves rippling across the battered landscape. The roar of explosions mixed with the clatter of machine-gun fire, a cacophony of war that seemed to have no beginning and no end.

Through this storm of destruction, Rommel's Panzer Corps surged forward, their steel beasts grinding through the ruined earth, engines growling like hungry predators. Tank tracks tore into the blackened soil, crushing the remains of trees and abandoned Soviet fortifications as they advanced toward the heart of Smolensk's defenses.

Inside his command Panzer IV, Rommel leaned forward, binoculars raised, scanning the battlefield ahead. His expression was calm, his gaze sharp, but even he could see it now—the Soviets had turned Smolensk into a fortress.

The Dnieper River, which cut through the region, had been reinforced with anti-tank barriers and machine-gun nests, the high ground beyond lined with Soviet artillery batteries. And beyond that, Rommel could just make out the silhouettes of Soviet T-34 tanks, their turrets shifting slowly, hunting for targets.

This was their last stand before Moscow.

A staff officer clambered up the side of the tank, gripping the edge of the turret to steady himself. His uniform was streaked with dirt, his face tight with tension.

"Herr General," he called over the deafening roar of the battle, "reports confirm Soviet positions are stronger than expected. Artillery emplacements along the Dnieper are slowing our advance."

Rommel didn't lower the binoculars.

Of course, they had made their stand here. Smolensk was their last natural defense line before Moscow. If the Germans punched through here, the road to the Soviet capital would be wide open.

"Strong defenses won't save them," Rommel said simply.

His gloved fingers tightened slightly on the edge of the hatch.

"Order all units to press forward. No delays."

The officer gave a quick nod, then slid back down the hull, vanishing into the chaos to man the radio lines.

Rommel watched for another moment, his mind already several steps ahead of the battle, calculating where to push hardest, where to exploit the inevitable Soviet collapse.

Then, with a final nod, he snapped his binoculars shut.

The Wehrmacht's full weight crashed against Smolensk's defenses.

II. Soviet Desperation

(June 11, 1941 – Smolensk, Soviet Command Bunker)

The command bunker beneath Smolensk trembled as another explosion shook the bunker. Dust rained from the ceiling. The walls groaned under relentless German artillery. The stone floors rumbled. Overhead lamps cast shadows over exhausted Soviet officers.

Marshal Semyon Timoshenko, his uniform streaked with sweat and grime, gripped the war table. His sharp, tired eyes locked onto the map before him.

Red markers—Soviet divisions—were disappearing. Swallowed by black and gray markers of German armor.

The room was silent.

Timoshenko's jaw tightened.

"We have to hold." His voice was low. Rough.

No one answered.

They all knew the truth.

Smolensk could not be held.

The Blitzkrieg had torn through Soviet defenses. Entire divisions were trapped before they could retreat. Supply lines shattered. Roads clogged with burning convoys. Communications severed.

Every message from the front was worse than the last.

The Red Army was being outmaneuvered. Outgunned. Outflanked.

And worst of all—the Luftwaffe owned the skies.

Supply depots. Railways. Reinforcements.

All bombed before they could reach the city.

There would be no rescue.

The bunker's steel door swung open. A junior officer stumbled in, covered in dust, snapping a salute.

"Comrade Marshal," he gasped, urgency in his voice, "the Germans are across the Dnieper. We cannot contain them."

Timoshenko's fists clenched at his sides.

He stared at the map, willing it to show him something—anything.

Nothing.

"Then hold what you can," he said at last. His voice was iron, but behind it, hollow.

"Every day we delay them is another day for Moscow to prepare."

But he knew—there weren't many days left.

III. Rommel's Breakthrough
(June 13, 1941 — Smolensk Outskirts, Wehrmacht Forward Lines)

The moment had come.

Standing atop a grassy ridge, Rommel surveyed Smolensk—or what remained of it. The once-thriving city was now a smoldering ruin. The glow of distant fires flickered against the morning haze, giving the war-torn streets an almost otherworldly glow.

Below him, his Panzer Corps lay poised, steel beasts lined up in perfect formation, their dark hulls reflecting the ghostly light of destruction. The battle had already pushed the Soviets back—the defensive lines along the Dnieper had collapsed, and with them, the last major obstacle between the Germans and the city itself.

The radio on his belt crackled, breaking the early morning stillness.

"Herr General," came the voice of a forward scout, "the Soviets are retreating into the city. They're preparing for street fighting."

Rommel's jaw tightened. He had fought in cities before. Urban combat was slow, brutal, and costly — a street-by-street, building-by-building fight where defenders had every advantage. It would drain time, resources, and men, and Rommel had neither to spare.

If he hesitated now, the Soviets would dig in, fortify the city, and turn Smolensk into a meat grinder.

He exhaled sharply, his icy blue eyes narrowing.

"We will not let them dig in."

He turned to his officers, his voice calm but absolute.

"Full assault. We take Smolensk today."

For a brief moment, silence hung over the ridge.

Then—thousands of German engines roared to life, the sound shaking the very earth beneath them.

Moments later, Rommel's Panzers surged forward, rolling down the slopes like an unstoppable wave of iron and fire, their guns blazing as they descended upon Smolensk.

IV. The City Burns
(June 14–16, 1941 – Smolensk, USSR)

The heart of Smolensk had grown eerily quiet. Fires still smoldered. The deafening explosions had faded in the distance.

The once-bustling streets lay deserted, covered in soot and shattered glass. Somewhere in the ruins, a dog barked—one sharp cry, then silence.

The only sound was the rhythmic crunch of German boots.

Rommel's Panzers and Wehrmacht infantry moved street by street, unstoppable. Soviet barricades collapsed under their relentless, mechanical advance.

The Red Army fought back viciously.

Riflemen crouched behind rubble, firing until their last bullet.

CASCADING DIVERGENCE 1941 Lebensraum

Machine gunners sprayed lead from the remains of ruined apartments.

Snipers lurked in the shadows, hunting German officers.

But nothing could stop the German war machine.

A Soviet lieutenant, barely out of officer school, stood on a pile of rubble, his face streaked with sweat and grime. His uniform was torn. His hands trembled as he shouted orders to men who were no longer there.

"Hold your ground! Hold—"

The order was never finished.

A Panzer shell screamed through the air.

The explosion erased him. One second, he stood. The next, he was dust and blood against the flames.

For three days, Smolensk burned.

Flamethrowers swept through Soviet holdouts, turning basements into infernos.

Grenades bounced through shattered windows, turning rooms into fire and molten steel.

By June 16, the last Soviet strongholds—factories, government buildings, rail stations—were falling one by one.

Morale was gone.

Ammunition was gone.

Reinforcements were never coming.

Inside a half-demolished warehouse, Marshal Timoshenko stood over a bloodstained map. His face was pale. His hands trembled.

A radio operator, uniform covered in soot and ash, approached. His voice was hoarse.

"Comrade Marshal… We cannot hold. Smolensk is lost."

Timoshenko closed his eyes. He exhaled slowly.

Then, without hesitation, he turned to his aide.

"Signal Moscow. The evacuation begins now."

V. Stalin's Reaction
(June 17, 1941 – Kremlin, Moscow)

The room was deathly silent.

Josef Stalin sat silently, his fingers steepled beneath his chin, his gaze locked on nothing—yet on everything. The glow of a half-smoked pipe flickered faintly in the dim light, the embers pulsing with each slow breath he took. Around him, the members of his inner circle waited, the air thick with unspoken fear.

Marshal Zhukov sat rigidly across from him, his uniform crumpled with exhaustion, dark circles beneath his eyes. Molotov, the Foreign Minister, held his hands clasped in his lap, his expression unreadable. Beria, head of the NKVD, lounged in his chair with an unnatural ease, but his eyes flickered restlessly. At the far end of the room sat Marshal Timoshenko, freshly returned from the front, his face drained of color.

CASCADING DIVERGENCE 1941 Lebensraum

None of them dared to speak first.

The map in front of them told the story they had all tried to ignore. Smolensk had fallen. A great hole gaped in the Soviet lines, Army Group Center pressing toward Vyazma—the last major obstacle before Moscow.

Finally, Zhukov spoke.

"Comrade Stalin, Smolensk has fallen."

The words hung in the air, settling like dust in a ruined city.

"The Germans are advancing toward Vyazma," he continued, his voice carefully measured. "If their momentum continues, they will reach the outskirts of Moscow within weeks."

A muscle in Stalin's jaw twitched, the only sign of tension on his otherwise impassive face. His grip on the table tightened, the wood groaning slightly under the pressure of his fingers.

"Then we will stop them there."

The room did not relax.

Zhukov hesitated, his throat dry. That was not a certainty.

"Comrade Stalin," he began again, choosing his words carefully, "the Germans are moving faster than they did in France. They are days ahead of their own schedule. We need time to build a proper defense."

Beria watched in silence, his eyes calculating, waiting to see if Stalin would lash out.

Stalin's face darkened, his gaze like steel.

"Time is a luxury we no longer have."

No one spoke.

The Soviet Union's capital was in danger—for the first time in history.

VI. Road to Moscow is Open
(June 20, 1941 – Wehrmacht Forward Command, Near Vyazma)

The morning sun cast a dull golden glow over the dust-choked roads, stretching toward Moscow like veins running to the heart of an empire. Rommel stood beside his mud-splattered staff car, arms folded, his sharp blue eyes scanning the horizon ahead.

There was nothing in the way.

Smolensk had fallen faster than even he had anticipated. The Soviet defenses had crumbled like rotted wood, their desperate counterattacks crushed, their retreat a chaotic stampede toward Moscow. Rommel could feel it—the city was within reach.

A motorcycle engine growled in the distance, a plume of dust trailing behind as the courier sped toward him. The rider dismounted swiftly, his boots crunching on the gravel, and snapped to attention, holding out a sealed message.

"From Field Marshal von Bock, Herr General."

Rommel took the paper, unfolding it with practiced precision. His eyes skimmed the message, his expression unreadable. Then, with a slight curl of his lips, he folded it neatly and tucked it into the inner pocket of his field coat.

CASCADING DIVERGENCE 1941 Lebensraum

"Hold positions and await further orders."

A long silence followed. Rommel knew why von Bock was hesitating. The generals at Army Group Center would want to regroup, refuel, and consolidate their lines before making the final push. It was logical. Cautious.

It was also a mistake.

Hesitation was the enemy of victory.

Rommel turned to his radio operator, his voice calm but firm.

"Prepare the men." He paused, glancing once more toward the open road ahead, toward the unconquered city beyond the horizon.

"We move forward at dawn."

RON WOOD

CASCADING DIVERGENCE 1941 Lebensraum

11

Drive to Moscow
June 21–Late July 1941 – Soviet Western Front, Russia

I. Germans Push Forward Without Delay
(June 21–30, 1941 – Wehrmacht Forward Command, Vyazma)

The blackened wreckage of Soviet vehicles littered the roads, twisted metal and charred bodies marking the path of Army Group Center. The push toward Moscow was relentless, an iron tide sweeping across the land, crushing anything that remained in its way.

Through the dust-choked air, columns of German Panzers roared eastward, the engines growling, the steel beasts advancing without hesitation. Every kilometer gained tightened the noose around the Soviets, pushing them toward inevitable collapse.

At the head of the formation, General Rommel stood atop the turret of his command tank, the wind whipping at his coat. He adjusted his binoculars, his sharp eyes scanning the road ahead. Vyazma loomed in the distance—a crucial waypoint on the road to Moscow. His men were exhausted, their rations dwindling, but there was no time to stop.

From below, the clang of boots on metal signaled an approaching messenger. A young staff officer climbed onto the tank, saluting crisply.

"Herr General, Field Marshal von Bock is ordering us to consolidate positions before advancing further."

Rommel's smirk was faint but unmistakable. He lowered the binoculars, fixing the officer with a knowing glance.

"Tell von Bock we are consolidating at Vyazma."

The officer hesitated, confused. "Sir, we haven't taken Vyazma yet."

Rommel's smirk widened. He turned back toward the horizon, where Soviet resistance was thinning by the hour. The city would be theirs soon enough.

"We will soon enough."

As he spoke, a deep rumble echoed in the distance—the engines of Guderian's 2nd Panzer Group and Hoth's 3rd Panzer Group, their formations pushing just as aggressively as Rommel's.

Neither would allow the Ghost Division to claim the lead unchallenged.

II. Rivalry Among the Panzer Commanders
(July 1–10, 1941 – Army Group Center, Russian Front)

The roads eastward were a frenzied blur of steel and dust, the momentum of Army Group Center now driven by something more than just orders—it was personal.

CASCADING DIVERGENCE 1941 Lebensraum

At his field headquarters, General Heinz Guderian paced beside a map table, his fingers pressed into the surface, his expression dark. Reports had been streaming in—Rommel had pushed even farther ahead, deeper into Soviet territory.

"Rommel's tactics are reckless," Guderian muttered, his voice edged with frustration. "If he keeps pushing without securing his flanks, he'll get himself cut off."

Across from him, his chief of staff remained silent for a moment before clearing his throat. "Sir, our reconnaissance suggests the Soviets don't have the strength to stop him."

Guderian's laugh was dry and humorless. "They didn't have the strength to stop me in France either, and I still used my damned head."

The truth was, as much as Guderian resented Rommel's reckless speed, he also envied it. The Ghost Division was making history again, and if Rommel seized Moscow first, it would be his victory alone. That, Guderian would not allow.

Miles away, Hoth, commanding the 3rd Panzer Group, had the same realization.

Standing on the turret of his tank, Hoth's eyes narrowed as he read a fresh dispatch. Rommel had broken through yet another Soviet line, pushing past Vyazma with alarming speed. If he continued at this rate, he'd reach Moscow first—an honor that belonged to all of Army Group Center, not just one man.

Hoth gritted his teeth.

"Signal all units. No delays. We match his speed."

The race to Moscow was no longer just a campaign.

It was a battle between generals, a contest where glory and history would favor the one who got there first.

But the faster they moved, the thinner their supply lines stretched.

And somewhere ahead, deep in Soviet territory, the Red Army was beginning to regroup.

III. Army Group North Nears Leningrad
(July 5–15, 1941 – Baltic Front, Estonia & Leningrad Oblast)

The summer sun hung low over the battlefields of the Baltic, casting long shadows over the burning remnants of Soviet defenses. Smoke curled into the sky, a silent testament to the relentless advance of Army Group North.

Inside his field headquarters, Field Marshal Wilhelm von Leeb stood over a large map, tracing the red arrows that marked his forces' rapid progress. The campaign through the Baltic states had been unstoppable—Riga had fallen on May 30, and by mid-July, the Wehrmacht had pushed deep into Estonia, the Soviet defenses crumbling before them.

But now, the first signs of real resistance were appearing.

An intelligence officer entered, wiping sweat from his brow. "Herr Feldmarschall, the Soviets are fortifying Leningrad."

Von Leeb's jaw tightened. He knew what this meant.

The city had massive industrial capacity, a population willing to fight, and a deep historical significance for the Soviets. If given enough time, Stalin would turn Leningrad into a fortress.

"Then we must strike before they are ready." His voice was calm, but his steel-gray eyes betrayed urgency.

IV. Army Group South Battles for Ukraine
(July 5–15, 1941 – Ukraine Front, Near Kiev & Kharkov)

The fields of Ukraine were alive with fire and steel. Smoke rose in thick columns, darkening the sky over the burning cities of Kiev and Kharkov, where the Red Army was making its last stand.

Inside his headquarters near Kiev, Field Marshal Gerd von Rundstedt stood with his hands clasped behind his back, his piercing blue eyes scanning the latest battle reports. Unlike the rapid collapse in Belarus, the Soviet forces in Ukraine were holding their ground.

"They are defending the cities well," von Rundstedt admitted. His voice was steady, but his brow furrowed as he studied the Soviet troop movements.

Unlike Rommel and Guderian, who had sliced through Soviet defenses in the north like a scalpel through flesh, the Wehrmacht in the south faced something different. Here, the Soviets were fighting like cornered wolves.

The streets of Kiev were a battlefield. Every intersection, every building, every underground tunnel had become a fortress. The Soviets had fortified their industrial cities, and what should have been a swift victory had turned into deadly urban warfare.

Von Rundstedt turned to his chief of staff. "And yet, they are still losing."

Despite the Soviet resistance, Army Group South was still advancing.

The reason? There were no reinforcements coming.

Every available Soviet division had been pulled north—Stalin had left Ukraine to its fate, sacrificing his southern armies in a desperate bid to defend Moscow.

Von Rundstedt allowed himself a rare smile of satisfaction.

"That was exactly what we wanted."

V. Stalin's Last Defensive Line
(July 15, 1941 – Kremlin, Moscow)

The Kremlin war room was a place where decisions shaped the fate of nations. The table was cluttered with maps, dispatches, and half-drunk cups of tea gone cold; the remnants of sleepless nights and desperate planning.

Josef Stalin stood motionless, his eyes focused on the thick red line marking Mozhaysk, the last defensive barrier before Moscow itself.

A mere 110 kilometers west of the capital.

"If we can hold them here, we can buy time," Zhukov's voice was firm, but fatigue lined his face. He had seen the reports. The Germans were coming faster than anyone had imagined—the Red Army was not stopping them, merely slowing them down.

CASCADING DIVERGENCE 1941 Lebensraum

Stalin exhaled, the weight of his own errors pressing down on him like a lead shroud.

For weeks, he had ignored the warnings. Had laughed at the idea of an invasion. Had dismissed intelligence reports as propaganda.

Now, Minsk was gone. Smolensk had fallen. The Red Army was broken.

He had once believed the Germans would never attack while they still needed Soviet oil. That belief had shattered along with the Soviet front lines.

For the first time, Stalin spoke with no delusions, no arrogance—only cold certainty.

"Hold the line."

His voice did not waver, though his heart pounded.

"Moscow will not fall."

But in the deepest corners of his mind, where he allowed no one to see, he knew the truth.

The Germans were coming.

VI. Hitler's Decision: No Diversion
(July 15, 1941 – Wolf's Lair, East Prussia)

The Wolf's Lair, Hitler's fortified headquarters in East Prussia, was stifling in the summer heat. Outside, the muffled sounds of radio transmissions and moving officers filled the air.

Inside, Germany's top military leaders had gathered. Field Marshal von Bock, General Halder, and other strategists sat ready for a critical discussion—one that would decide the next move in the campaign.

A detailed map of the Soviet Union was pinned to the wall, covered in black arrows, all leading to Moscow.

Von Bock stood, his hands resting on the table. His voice was firm.

"Mein Führer, we don't need to shift our forces south. The Soviets are already collapsing. Moscow is within reach."

Halder nodded in agreement.

"Army Group Center is advancing at an unprecedented pace, Mein Führer. Rommel and Guderian are near Mozhaysk. If we push now, Moscow will fall before winter."

Some officers exchanged glances. The discussion was clear—there was a chance to end the war quickly with a final strike.

All eyes turned to Hitler.

He steepled his fingers, staring at the map. His expression remained blank, unreadable.

For a long moment, the room was silent.

Finally, Hitler exhaled and spoke.

"Continue the advance."

A murmur spread through the room. The decision was made.

CASCADING DIVERGENCE 1941 Lebensraum

VII. Germans Reach the Outskirts of Moscow
(Late July 1941 – Near Moscow, Soviet Western Front)

The rumble of German Panzers filled the air as Army Group Center moved forward.

The skyline of Moscow was finally in sight.

Standing on his command tank, Rommel raised his binoculars. He scanned the city ahead. The Kremlin's domes glinted in the sunlight.

Behind him, Guderian's 2nd Panzer Group moved into position, their tanks kicking up dust as they prepared for the final push. To the north, Hoth's forces were closing in, cutting off any last chance for the Soviets to reinforce.

Rommel lowered his binoculars, a small, satisfied smile on his face.

"So," he muttered, "this is it."

The race to Moscow was over.

Now, the battle for the Soviet capital was about to begin.

RON WOOD

12

Siege of the Capital
Early August–Mid-August 1941 – Moscow, USSR

I. German Army Enters the City
(August 5, 1941 – Western Outskirts of Moscow)

Moscow was shrouded in an eerie twilight, even though the sun still hung in the sky. Fires burned unchecked, casting dancing shadows against the battered facades of Soviet apartment blocks. The once-proud Soviet capital, a city that had stood for centuries, was now on the brink of destruction.

A low, rolling thunder echoed across the city, the constant drumbeat of German artillery smashing into its western districts.

From his position atop a Panzer IV, Rommel raised his binoculars, scanning the broken skyline. He could see the jagged remains of factories and government buildings, their windows blown out, their walls riddled with shrapnel scars. In the distance, beyond the barricades and plumes of smoke, he could make out the spires of the Kremlin, still standing, defiant.

His radio operator handed him a fresh update.

"Herr General, Guderian's forces have entered the city from the south. Hoth's divisions are pressing in from the north."

Rommel lowered his binoculars, a smirk flickering across his dust-covered face.

"So the Reds want to fight in the streets?" he muttered.

The officer beside him hesitated. "Soviet resistance is stiffening, sir."

Rommel's expression darkened.

"Then we push harder."

His hand shot up, signaling the next phase of the assault.

Moments later, the entire weight of the Panzer Corps lurched forward, their treads grinding over shattered pavement, their guns primed for the brutal combat ahead.

II. Zhukov's Last Stand
(August 6, 1941 – Kremlin, Moscow)

In the Kremlin war room, Marshal Zhukov stood hunched over a massive, tattered map of the city that showed thin, red defensive lines that had once seemed formidable but were now crumbling beneath the weight of the German onslaught.

The Germans were inside the city.

He could hear the muffled sounds of gunfire from the Arbat district, where Soviet conscripts—many barely old enough to shave—were hurling Molotov cocktails at advancing German Panzers. They would hold for minutes, maybe an hour, but the outcome was inevitable.

CASCADING DIVERGENCE 1941 Lebensraum

Across the room, Stalin sat motionless in his chair, the glow of his pipe the only sign of life in his otherwise stony demeanor. He had barely spoken since the first reports of German tanks rolling through the western districts had come in. The Red Tsar, so often unshakable, now seemed haunted—as if watching history slip from his grasp in real-time.

Zhukov clenched his fists, forcing the rising frustration in his chest back down. He could not afford doubt. Not now.

"Comrade Stalin," he began, his voice gravelly, raw from exhaustion, "we still hold the city center, but we cannot stop their advance without reinforcements."

A long silence followed.

Stalin exhaled slowly, a thin plume of smoke curling above his head before dissipating into the heavy air.

"There are no reinforcements."

Zhukov's jaw tightened, the words landing with a dead weight in his chest. He had already known the truth, but hearing it aloud made it feel like the final nail in Moscow's coffin.

The Red Army had thrown everything it had into the fight, but it wasn't enough.

Zhukov swallowed hard. "Then—"

Stalin cut him off with a slow, deliberate look.

"Then we fight to the last man."

The room remained silent, but the meaning was unmistakable.

Moscow would not surrender.

They would burn the city to the ground before letting it fall into German hands.

III. Luftwaffe Over Moscow
(August 7–10, 1941 – Moscow Airspace)

The first Luftwaffe bombers came with the dawn.

From the Kremlin's battered defenses, the skyline was filled with silver glints reflecting the morning sun—hundreds of Heinkel He 111 bombers, their formations tight and disciplined, marching methodically through the sky toward the heart of the Soviet capital.

The drone of their engines was deafening, a low, constant hum that grew into a monstrous roar, drowning out the already chaotic sounds of Moscow's final defenses below.

From the ground, Soviet anti-aircraft gunners fought with desperate fury.

Bright flashes of flak bursts bloomed across the sky, black puffs of smoke dotting the heavens like ink stains. Tracer rounds sliced upward in scarlet streaks, wild and frantic, but the Germans kept coming.

Then came the bombs.

The first wave of ordnance fell like a steel rain, and Moscow shook beneath the impact.

CASCADING DIVERGENCE 1941 Lebensraum

The skyline erupted in pillars of flame, entire city blocks consumed in a matter of seconds. Rail depots collapsed under the crushing blasts. A munitions factory near the Moskva River detonated, sending shockwaves across the city. Bridges buckled, collapsing into the water below, and thick plumes of dust curled into the air, blotting out the sun.

Forward Wehrmacht Headquarters
(Outside Moscow, August 7, 1941 – 07:30 Hours)

From his command post west of the city, Rommel stood near a field radio, listening. The monotone voices of Luftwaffe pilots crackled through the receiver.

"Multiple targets hit. Firestorms spreading through central Moscow. No sign of organized resistance."

Another transmission, this one from a dive-bomber squadron:

"Flak is heavy, but ineffective. Bombing runs proceeding. Stalin's city burns."

Rommel exhaled, slowly. He looked over his shoulder, toward the distant orange glow of explosions illuminating the skyline.

The Soviet capital was bleeding, and he knew it wouldn't hold out much longer.

But something gnawed at him—the Soviets were still fighting.

A Suicide in the Sky
(Above Red Square, August 8, 1941 – 09:45 Hours)

Despite losing control of the skies, a handful of Soviet I-16 fighters still scrambled to meet the German bombers head-on.

They were outnumbered ten to one.

They launched anyway.

The tiny, aging aircraft climbed in desperate, erratic spirals, their pilots pushing their machines to the breaking point. Luftwaffe Messerschmitts were waiting, swooping in like falcons, picking them off one by one.

Still, they kept coming.

A Soviet pilot, his aircraft already riddled with bullets, saw a Heinkel bomber ahead, lumbering toward the Kremlin with its payload intact. He had no ammunition left, no way to shoot it down.

So he made a decision.

With a final yank of the control stick, he angled his nose straight into the bomber's fuselage.

The collision was instant and catastrophic.

The wreckage of both planes spun downward, twisting in flames, until—

They slammed into Red Square, exploding in a thunderous fireball.

The Soviet pilots were dying, but they were taking the enemy with them.

CASCADING DIVERGENCE 1941 Lebensraum

The Luftwaffe had air superiority—but Moscow still refused to surrender.

IV. Brutal Street Fighting
(August 10–15, 1941 – Moscow Streets)

The Wehrmacht had fought in cities before—but never like this.

Moscow was a trap. Collapsed buildings. Barricaded streets. Snipers in every shadow. The Red Army had turned the city into a killing ground.

German Panzers crept forward, iron hulls scraping against ruined buildings. Machine guns rattled from rooftops. Every window was a sniper's nest.

Inside his command tank, Rommel gritted his teeth.

This wasn't Paris. It wasn't even Warsaw.

The Soviets were fighting for every block. Every street. Every stone.

Through his binoculars, he spotted a German squad rounding a corner.

A burst of machine-gun fire tore through them. Bodies crumpled into the rubble.

Above, shadows moved behind shattered windows. A grenade tumbled from a balcony.

"Grenade!"

The explosion ripped through the street, sending dust and debris into the air.

Rommel grabbed his radio.

"Clear the buildings!"

The Wehrmacht pushed forward, but every inch was paid for in blood.

Flamethrowers spewed fire, forcing Soviet troops from their barricades.

Grenades bounced through shattered windows, clearing rooms one explosion at a time.

Inside a department store, Soviet defenders fought from behind overturned counters.

A young Soviet lieutenant, barely twenty, barked orders. His men were a mix of veterans and terrified conscripts.

A German grenade bounced into the room.

"Down!"

The explosion shredded half the defenders.

Before the survivors could react, German stormtroopers charged in—submachine guns blazing.

The lieutenant raised his pistol. Fired twice. Then a bullet hit his chest.

He staggered, falling against a shattered shelf.

Above, a Soviet sniper took aim.

His scope locked onto a German soldier.

He fired.

CASCADING DIVERGENCE 1941 Lebensraum

A Wehrmacht soldier collapsed, blood splattered on the wall behind him.

Before the sniper could fire again, a German tank shell smashed into his building.

The upper floors collapsed, burying him alive.

Moscow's defenders weren't just soldiers.

Factory workers. Old men. Teenagers.

Women hurled Molotov cocktails from rooftops.

In a narrow alley, a group of civilians ambushed a German patrol.

A Wehrmacht officer hit the ground. His helmet rolled away in the dirt.

A civilian lunged with a sharpened pipe.

A gunshot rang out.

The man collapsed, clutching his stomach.

The rest of the civilians scattered.

The fight was far from over.

Rommel studied the reports.

His troops had pushed deep into the city, but the Soviets weren't breaking.

They weren't just fighting for survival.

They were fighting with hatred so fierce, it defied logic.

He exhaled, watching smoke rise over the ruined skyline.

For the first time in the campaign, he felt it.

Moscow would not fall easily.

V. Stalin's Decision: Stay or Flee?
(August 15, 1941 – Kremlin, Moscow)

The walls of the Kremlin trembled as another German artillery shell exploded nearby, shaking the massive structure to its foundation.

Dust trickled from the ceiling, settling over the long, mahogany table where Stalin sat, motionless, his fingers drumming softly against the wood.

Outside, the muffled echoes of battle grew louder, the distant rattle of machine-gun fire and the booming of tank cannons creeping closer. The city, his city, was burning, and still, he refused to move.

Across the room, Vyacheslav Molotov and Lavrentiy Beria stood uneasily, their faces lined with exhaustion and something else—fear.

"Comrade Stalin," Molotov said at last, his voice carefully measured, "we must evacuate you to Kuybyshev. The city is collapsing."

Stalin did not answer immediately.

Instead, he slowly reached for his pipe, knocking out the ashes with precise, calculated taps against a ceramic tray. He refilled it deliberately, methodically, as if the entire city wasn't on the verge of total annihilation.

CASCADING DIVERGENCE 1941 Lebensraum

Then, without looking up, he spoke.

"No."

Molotov shifted uncomfortably.

"If they break through to Red Square—" he pressed, his voice betraying a hint of desperation.

Stalin finally looked up, his dark eyes locking onto Molotov's, unwavering, unshaken.

"Then I will fight from Red Square."

His voice was calm, as if he were discussing a minor bureaucratic matter, not the fall of the Soviet capital.

Beria, ever the opportunist, said nothing.

He already knew the truth.

Stalin would never abandon Moscow.

The war had not broken him.

And if the Germans wanted the Kremlin, they would have to pry it from his dead hands.

Outside, another shell screamed through the air, exploding just beyond the gates of the fortress.

The war was at his doorstep.

VI. Germans Close In
(August 16–18, 1941 – Moscow City Center)

The sun faded behind the blackened sky, once bright over the Soviet capital, now a dull, blood-red glow. The streets lay in ruin. Buildings stood as crumbling skeletons, their facades shredded by artillery fire. Statues of Lenin and Stalin lay buried beneath the rubble. The Wehrmacht had reached the last Soviet defenses.

From the west, Rommel's Panzers rumbled forward, crushing the last barricades beneath their steel treads. They moved with cold precision, slicing through Soviet resistance like a scalpel through flesh. From the south, Guderian's 2nd Panzer Group advanced methodically, cutting through Moscow's outer districts. The few Soviet defenders left fought like cornered wolves—but they were too few, too tired, too poorly armed. From the north, Hoth's 3rd Panzer Group closed in, severing Moscow's final supply routes. The city was being choked into submission. The Soviets were surrounded. There was nowhere left to run.

High above the ruined city, a Soviet rifleman crouched on a collapsed rooftop, his breath ragged, his hands shaking from exhaustion and fear. His uniform was filthy, his rifle worn. Through the twisting smoke, he saw them. The Germans were coming. Through the ruins of Tverskaya Street, Rommel's Panzers rolled forward, their gun barrels poised to finish the city. The soldier's fingers clenched the trigger. He knew one bullet wouldn't stop a tank. He knew his city was doomed.

But he took aim anyway.

13

Moscow Falls
Mid-August 1941 – Moscow, USSR

I. The City Burns
(August 18, 1941 – Moscow City Center)

Moscow was dying.

The sky was thick with the stench of burning flesh, gasoline, and gunpowder; a choking fog that seeped into every shattered street and ruined building. Once, the city had been the heart of the Soviet Union. Now, it was a corpse, crushed beneath the iron treads of German tanks.

In the ruins of a destroyed textile factory, Rommel stood on smoldering rubble, binoculars raised. His Panzers surged forward, engines howling, cannons spitting fire at the last Soviet defenders. The city was lost, but still, they fought.

He lowered his binoculars, eyes narrowing. The Soviets were pulling back, retreating toward Red Square.

A radio operator stumbled toward him, face streaked with sweat and soot. "Herr General!" he gasped. "Zhukov is making his final stand near the Kremlin!"

Rommel's jaw tightened. "Then this ends today."

He turned to his officers, his voice like iron. "All units—push forward."

The Wehrmacht surged ahead. Tanks crushed barricades beneath their treads. Infantry stormed through burning ruins, bayonets fixed, rifles ready.

II. Stalin's Last Orders
(August 18, 1941 – Kremlin, Moscow)

The Kremlin shook again, a deep, shuddering tremor that rattled the steel lamps above and sent a cascade of dust drifting from the vaulted ceiling.

But Stalin did not move.

He sat in the half-lit depths of his underground command center, the glow of the oil lamps casting sharp shadows across his gaunt, unshaven face.

Marshal Georgy Zhukov stood rigid, his uniform soaked in sweat, stained with soot and flecks of dried blood. He had not slept in two days. His face was drawn and pale, but his eyes still burned with raw defiance.

Outside, Moscow was dying.

Gunfire rattled through the streets above them, the sharp chatter of Soviet submachine guns met by the steady, disciplined bursts of German fire. The dull, distant roar of tank cannons echoed through the walls, like thunder announcing the coming storm.

Zhukov inhaled slowly, steadying his voice.

CASCADING DIVERGENCE 1941 Lebensraum

"Comrade Stalin," he said, his voice hoarse but firm. "Our forces are nearly spent. The Germans will breach Red Square within hours."

A moment of silence.

Stalin's fingers tapped idly against the scarred surface of the table.

Then, in a voice as cold as steel, he murmured:

"Then we fight in the streets."

Molotov, standing stiffly to the side, shifted uneasily. His glasses caught the dim light as he wiped his damp hands on his coat.

"Comrade Stalin… if the Germans capture the Kremlin—"

Stalin's eyes snapped up.

"They will not."

For the first time, he looked up fully, his gaze hard, unshaken, unbreakable.

Outside, the walls rattled again as another Luftwaffe bomb hit somewhere nearby, sending a tremor through the stone floors.

Yet Stalin remained utterly still.

"Issue the final orders," he commanded, his voice low but firm.

His cold gaze swept across the room, daring anyone to defy him.

"Any soldier who surrenders will be executed. We fight to the last man."

A final, heavy silence settled over the room.

Zhukov's jaw clenched, his hands curling into fists at his sides. He did not argue. There was nothing left to say.

The order was given.

III. Luftwaffe Destroys the Defenses
(August 19, 1941 – Over Moscow)

The sky was black with bombers.

At precisely 05:00 hours, the first wave of Heinkel He 111s appeared on the horizon, their dark silhouettes barely visible against the smoke-clogged morning sky. They flew in tight, disciplined formations, engines droning in an eerie mechanical hum, the sound of death descending upon the city.

The Kremlin's anti-aircraft batteries opened fire.

The first bursts of flak exploded in the sky like black flowers, peppering the air with shrapnel. Soviet gunners, operating with scorched hands and empty stomachs, worked furiously to keep up the fire, their guns overheating, barrels warping, their ammunition reserves dwindling fast.

It wasn't enough.

The Luftwaffe owned the sky now.

Then came the bombs.

CASCADING DIVERGENCE 1941 Lebensraum

The first detonations shattered the silence, sending shockwaves through the Kremlin's stone walls. The ground trembled as ancient structures cracked open, releasing torrents of swirling ash and flickering flames that lit up the chaos.

More bombers appeared from the west.

Junkers Ju 88s and Dornier Do 17s swooped in low, their payloads falling in deadly succession. They aimed for the last Soviet strongholds, obliterating command posts, artillery batteries, and hastily constructed barricades.

The Kremlin's anti-aircraft guns fell silent.

A massive explosion rocked the Senate Building, its roof caving in as the Luftwaffe finished the job.

Inside his cockpit, Oberleutnant Klaus Reinhardt adjusted his controls, banking his Heinkel slightly to the left, his eyes narrowing as he surveyed the destruction below.

Flames engulfed Red Square. The golden domes of St. Basil's Cathedral were barely visible through the thick smoke curling into the air.

Reinhardt's lips curled into a smirk.

He keyed his radio.

"Target eliminated," he reported.

As he pulled his aircraft into a slow turn, he glanced once more toward the ruins of the Kremlin and muttered under his breath:

"Berlin will be celebrating tonight."

IV. Germans Enter Red Square
(August 19, 1941 – Red Square, Moscow)

The tanks rolled forward.

At 12:07 PM, the first Panzer IVs entered Red Square, crushing what was left of the barricades and debris. Dust and soot covered their hulls, streaking their camouflage. Behind them, Wehrmacht infantry marched in formation, scanning the area for any last resistance.

The Soviet capital was falling.

From his command half-track, Rommel watched through his binoculars as his troops secured the square. Spasskaya Tower loomed ahead, its shattered clock face frozen in time.

To the south, Guderian's tanks moved through the damaged streets, breaking through the last Soviet positions. To the north, Hoth's troops blocked any possible escape routes.

A burst of gunfire cut through the air.

A Soviet machine gun, hidden inside a damaged shop, opened fire. German soldiers fell instantly, their weapons clattering to the ground.

Rommel ducked behind cover, shaking his head.

"Take out that nest!" he ordered.

A flamethrower team moved in, covered by rifle squads. The flamethrower hissed, then sent fire into the shop.

The gunfire stopped.

Rommel exhaled, scanning the square.

CASCADING DIVERGENCE 1941 Lebensraum

Red Square was almost secured.

Above, Reich banners flapped in the wind. The last Soviet defenses were falling, and with them, the final hopes of Moscow's defenders.

V. Stalin's Fate
(August 19, 1941 – Kremlin, Moscow)

The Kremlin was in flames.

The last Red Army soldiers fought on, their bullets cutting through the dust-filled air. One by one, they fell beneath the advancing Wehrmacht.

Marshal Georgy Zhukov, his uniform torn and bloodied, stood in a dim hallway, firing his Tokarev pistol as German troops stormed in.

"Hold the line! Hold the line!" he shouted.

His men kept falling.

It was over.

Beyond the shattered windows, Red Square belonged to the Reich. The Kremlin, once a symbol of Soviet power, had become a tomb. Empty shell casings clattered on the marble floors. The wounded gasped for breath. German boots marched forward.

Inside his office, Stalin sat motionless.

The flames had not reached him yet.

A pistol rested beside his hand. Untouched.

The clock ticked.

A Soviet officer burst into the room, his uniform torn, his face pale.

"Comrade Stalin, the Germans—"

The doors flew open.

A Wehrmacht squad stormed in, rifles raised.

A young officer stepped forward.

"Joseph Stalin, by order of the German Reich, you are under arrest."

Stalin didn't move.

His fingers rested on the desk. His face remained unreadable.

He exhaled slowly. His eyes flicked to the gun beside him.

But he did not reach for it.

He simply leaned back in his chair.

And just like that, it was over.

VI. Moscow Falls
(August 20, 1941 – German High Command, Moscow)

The Reich war flag flapped harshly in the wind above the Kremlin, its crimson cloth soaked in the golden glow of the morning sun. Below it, the battered ruins of Moscow lay in smoking devastation, its streets strewn with the broken bodies of the fallen, its buildings reduced to hollowed-out husks.

CASCADING DIVERGENCE 1941 Lebensraum

Moscow had fallen.

Rommel stood amid the wreckage of Red Square, his dust-covered uniform stiff with sweat, his boots gritting against shattered stone and glass. His gloved hands gripped his binoculars, but he barely needed them—there was no battle left to see.

The Red Army was gone.

Behind him, the once-majestic domes of St. Basil's Cathedral were marred by bullet holes, its mosaics shattered. The towers of the Kremlin, symbols of Soviet power, stood defaced and blackened.

Gunfire popped in the distance, but it was scattered and desperate, nothing more than the last gasps of a crushed enemy.

A Wehrmacht officer approached, his boots clicking against the stone. He saluted.

"Herr General, Field Marshal von Bock is awaiting your report."

Rommel let out a measured breath, his sharp blue eyes surveying the conquered capital.

He could still smell the burning flesh from the pyres where Soviet bodies had been piled high. The stench of gunpowder and ruin clung to the air like a death shroud.

He turned to the officer, his voice calm but final.

"Tell von Bock that Moscow is ours."

A pause.

His lips curled into a subtle smirk, but there was no arrogance in it—just the pragmatic satisfaction of a soldier who had completed his mission.

CASCADING DIVERGENCE 1941 Lebensraum

14

Aftermath of the Fall
Late August–December 1941 – Moscow & Beyond

I. Soviet Leadership Forced to Surrender
(August 23, 1941 – Moscow, Under German Control)

The streets of Moscow were silent. Once the center of Soviet power, the city lay in ruins. Rubble and bodies filled the streets. Fires still smoldered.

In Red Square, the Reich war flag fluttered where the Soviet hammer and sickle had once flown. German soldiers patrolled the shattered avenues, boots echoing against the broken stone. They stepped over collapsed buildings, burned-out vehicles, and fallen Soviet soldiers.

The war in the East was over.

Inside the former Soviet Ministry of Defense, now a German command center, a long table stretched across the dimly lit room.

On one side sat Josef Stalin, Vyacheslav Molotov, and Lavrentiy Beria. Their uniforms were torn and filthy. Their faces were gaunt, their expressions unreadable.

On the other side stood the conquerors.

At the head of the room, Field Marshal Fedor von Bock held a document in his hands. His posture was rigid, his gaze cold. He did not gloat. He did not smile. He was here to finish history.

His voice was sharp, precise.

"This agreement officially dissolves the Soviet Union and transfers all former Soviet territories to the Greater German Reich. Effective immediately, all Soviet military forces are to disband. Any claims to governance from your so-called Soviet state are null and void."

A German interpreter repeated the words in Russian, his tone flat, mechanical.

No one spoke.

Molotov reached for the pen first. His hand trembled as he signed. There was no hesitation. There was nothing left to negotiate.

Beria followed. He paused, glancing at Stalin. The usual scowl was gone. His predatory arrogance had vanished. He looked small. He signed.

Then, all eyes turned to Stalin.

The dictator sat motionless. He stared at the paper.

He did not move.

The silence thickened.

A German officer stepped forward. His voice was quiet. Not a request.

CASCADING DIVERGENCE 1941 Lebensraum

"Sign, Comrade Stalin."

A long moment passed.

For a second—just a second—it seemed he might refuse. He might spit in defiance, throw the pen aside, force them to execute him on the spot.

But then, slowly, deliberately, Stalin reached forward.

His hand did not shake.

The pen scratched across the page. His signature was a black scar against history.

And just like that, it was done.

The Soviet Union was no more.

II. Fall of Leningrad
(August 25–September 15, 1941 – Leningrad Front, Northern Russia)

With Moscow fallen, Leningrad stood alone.

For weeks, the city had endured a relentless siege, its defenders stretched thin, its people starving, its hope fading. Now, the end had come.

Field Marshal Wilhelm von Leeb, commander of Army Group North, stood atop a makeshift observation platform, staring toward Leningrad's broken skyline.

He lowered his binoculars. The time for siege was over.

"Begin the final assault," he ordered.

The Luftwaffe had already done its work.

For days, squadrons of Heinkel bombers had rained destruction upon the city. Supply depots, communication centers, bridges, and food storage facilities had been reduced to ash and rubble. Leningrad's lifelines had been cut, its people left to rot in their bombed-out homes and shattered streets.

There was no clean death here.

Water lines had ruptured. The food reserves were gone. Civilians, once the proud workers of the Soviet industrial heartland, withered away in the shadows, their bodies thin and brittle as autumn leaves. The dead lay unburied, their corpses stripped for clothing, their meat stolen in the night.

The city's defenders, both soldiers and civilians alike, clung to life with desperate tenacity. But desperation is not a shield, and starvation is not a weapon.

The Germans advanced, pushing through fortified buildings, clearing sniper nests, reducing barricades to dust.

Inside the besieged city, Major General Ivan Fedyuninsky, the acting commander of Leningrad's defenses, stood in the ruined remains of the Smolny Institute, once a center of Bolshevik power. He wiped the blood from a gash on his forehead, his uniform stained with soot and sweat.

A young officer rushed into the room.

"Comrade General!" he gasped. "The Germans have reached the Admiralty! Our lines are collapsing!"

Fedyuninsky said nothing at first. He already knew.

CASCADING DIVERGENCE 1941 Lebensraum

Outside, the booming of German artillery was deafening. The last Red Army positions were being overrun, their bunkers caving in, their machine-gun nests falling silent, one by one.

A few ragged defenders still fought, hurling grenades from windows, ambushing German patrols, dragging the wounded into darkened alleyways. But it wasn't enough. It would never be enough.

The young officer swallowed hard. His hands shook, his eyes hollow.

"What are your orders, Comrade General?"

Fedyuninsky turned toward the tattered Soviet flag still hanging over his command post.

"We hold," he said.

But even as he spoke the words, he knew Leningrad was lost.

On September 15, 1941, under the gray autumn sky, Leningrad surrendered.

The last of its Red Army defenders laid down their weapons, their faces gaunt, their bodies broken.

As Wehrmacht officers marched into the city's center, they found a world already dead. Streets filled with the skeletal remains of its people, shattered factories, ruined monuments, and silence where there had once been defiance.

A Reich war banner was raised over the Winter Palace, flapping in the cold wind.

Germany now controlled Russia's two greatest cities—Moscow and Leningrad.

III. Conquest of the Caucasus
(September–October 1941 – Southern Front, Caucasus & Ukraine)

The fall of Moscow and Leningrad had shattered what was left of Soviet command. The Red Army was in full retreat, leaderless and broken.

Army Group South, under Field Marshal von Rundstedt, now set its sights on the Caucasus. Germany had not only defeated the Soviet Union—it was about to take control of its most valuable resource.

With no orders from Moscow, Soviet forces in Ukraine and the Caucasus collapsed. Entire divisions, left without direction or reinforcements, either disbanded, fled, or surrendered. Few wanted to fight for a dead regime.

Soviet commanders who had once defended Kiev and Kharkov now faced a choice—fight and be wiped out, or surrender and survive. Thousands chose surrender.

And still, the German advance didn't stop.

The Luftwaffe launched one of its most devastating air campaigns. Bombers hit rail hubs, bridges, fuel depots, and industrial centers, ensuring the last remnants of Soviet resistance were cut off.

Partisans tried to destroy the oil fields before the Germans could reach them.

But they were too slow.

CASCADING DIVERGENCE 1941 Lebensraum

The Wehrmacht struck first, sending sabotage teams alongside armored spearheads. Every pipeline, refinery, and well the Soviets planned to destroy was secured before they could act.

On October 12, 1941, German forces entered Baku.

Once the crown jewel of Soviet industry, the oil-rich city had fueled Stalin's war machine.

Now, it belonged to the Reich.

Wehrmacht tanks rolled through the streets, their tracks grinding over broken pavement. German soldiers hoisted the Reich war banner over Baku's massive refineries.

German engineers moved in immediately. Pumping stations were secured. The flow of crude oil to the Reich was guaranteed.

Germany would never run out of fuel again. Its Panzers would no longer be limited by rationing.

With Baku in German hands, Hitler now had what had eluded him in the past—an unlimited fuel supply.

By late October, Germany had achieved every major objective.

The entire western Soviet Union—from the Baltic to the Black Sea, from the Volga to the Caucasus—was under German rule.

The Reich was now an empire, stretching from the Atlantic to the Caspian Sea.

The war, it seemed, was over. Germany had won.

IV. Hitler's Inner Circle Debates Siberia
(November 1941 – Führer Headquarters, Berlin)

The Reich had achieved the unthinkable—the conquest of Moscow, Leningrad, and the Caucasus.

With the Soviet Union shattered, there was no enemy left to fight.

The question was no longer how to win the war—but how to rule what they had won.

Yet, even in victory, Hitler's inner circle was divided.

The debate began with one question—what would become of Siberia?

At the Wolfsschanze, Hitler's fortified headquarters in East Prussia, Germany's most powerful leaders gathered.

Hitler sat in silence, his steely blue eyes scanning the faces of his generals, ministers, and officials.

There were no more battle plans. No urgent reports from the Eastern Front.

Only one question remained—what now?

Himmler leaned forward first. His gloved fingers tapped against the table.

"Mein Führer, we must push into Siberia. The East is ours—let us take all of it!"

His voice brimmed with excitement.

CASCADING DIVERGENCE 1941 Lebensraum

"Siberia is vast, rich in resources. We should begin immediate German settlement! Villages, highways, railroads—our empire must expand to the Pacific!"

His eyes gleamed as he continued.

"We will cleanse the land of undesirables. The Reich's borders should not stop at Moscow, but at Vladivostok!"

The room fell silent.

Then, a scoff.

Göring leaned back in his chair, a sneer twisting across his broad face.

"Himmler, have you ever actually seen a map?"

Himmler's face twitched, but he said nothing.

Göring's tone was amused.

"Siberia is nothing but forests, frozen rivers, and wolves. And you want to build settlements? Where? In the permafrost?"

A few generals exchanged glances. None spoke.

Göring waved a hand.

"We don't need to waste men and steel on another conquest. We already have everything—grain from Ukraine, oil from Baku, Russian factories working for us. Let the locals mine our resources. Siberia is an afterthought."

His eyes turned to Hitler, his voice calmer now.

"Mein Führer, our focus should be consolidating what we've won, not chasing ghosts in the East."

At the far end of the table, General Franz Halder sat with his fingers laced together.

He had remained silent. Until now.

"A campaign in Siberia would be a logistical nightmare."

His voice was calm, without emotion.

"We have stretched our supply lines to their limit. Our troops are already enduring the Russian winter. If we push further, into lands with no cities, no roads, no infrastructure, we will be fighting against nature itself."

His eyes met Hitler's.

"Mein Führer, if we go farther, we will not be fighting a war. We will be marching into the abyss."

The room fell silent.

All eyes turned to Hitler, who had not spoken since the discussion began.

His elbows rested on the table, fingers pressed together, gaze locked on the maps before him.

At last, he leaned back in his chair. His voice was quiet but final.

"We have everything we need."

His gaze swept the room, daring anyone to challenge him.

CASCADING DIVERGENCE 1941 Lebensraum

"The East belongs to us. Moscow, Leningrad, Baku—the Bolsheviks are finished. The Reich has already won."

He let the words settle.

Then, he turned to Himmler.

"Siberia can wait."

The Reich's focus would not be on frozen wastelands—but on securing what it had already taken.

For now.

V. Hitler Declares Total Victory
(Early December 1941 – Berlin, Germany)

On December 5, Hitler addressed the world in a historic radio broadcast:

Sons and daughters of the Reich, history has been rewritten. The German soldier no longer fights in the East—the war is won. The Bolshevik beast is dead. Europe is free from its corruption. What began as a test of our will has ended in a victory that will echo for generations. This is the day we declare our final triumph over Bolshevism. This is VB Day!

You, the German people, have endured, sacrificed, and fought for this moment. Your loyalty, your perseverance, your faith in the Reich have ensured Germany's rightful place as the master of Europe. You stood firm against war, against the lies of our enemies, and now, you reap the rewards. Our lands are secure. Our future unchallenged. The blood and iron of the German people have forged an empire that shall endure for a thousand years!

To the people of the East, to those once trapped under Bolshevism—Stalin was never your savior. He was your oppressor. He bled you dry. He sent your kin to the gulags. He executed your own officers. You were not citizens of a great empire—you were prisoners of a dying state. But that time is over. The Reich has shattered your chains, and for the first time in decades, your future is no longer dictated by fear and lies.

Bolshevism is dead, but the Russian people are not. To those in Moscow, Leningrad, Ukraine, and Siberia, hear this—Germany does not seek your destruction. We bring stability, order, prosperity. The terror of Stalin's regime is over. A new future awaits you. Work, tend to your families, follow the directives of your new administrators. Those who contribute will find security. There will be no chaos, only transition. Those who cooperate will see the benefits of discipline and stability under German rule.

To the world leaders who doubted us—look at Germany now. We conquered because we were strong. We triumphed because we were right. But we do not seek war for war's sake. Nations beyond our borders need not fear the Reich. Our aims are fulfilled. We have taken what is rightfully ours. The Reich has restored order, replaced barbarism with civilization, and turned uncertainty into destiny. Let this victory mark not just the end of Bolshevism, but the beginning of a stable Europe—one led by the Reich, one that will never again be corrupted by the past.

To our soldiers, our workers, every man, woman, and child who made this victory possible—the Reich salutes you. The banners of Germany fly over the Kremlin, and with them, a new order begins. The sacrifices of today will be honored for eternity. On every VB Day, we will remember this moment—when Europe was freed, when Germany stood victorious, when our destiny was fulfilled.

The future belongs to those who build it with strength, discipline, and vision. Today is not the end of struggle, but the beginning of an era of stability, prosperity, and order. A new chapter in history has begun, and Germany stands at its heart. May this peace endure as the foundation of a greater tomorrow. Heil Deutschland!

VI. Christmas Eve Celebration
(December 24, 1941 – Berlin, Germany)

Good evening, Germany. This is Radio Berlin, and tonight, history is being made. The war is over. Victory is ours.

I wish you could see what I see right now. The streets of Berlin are packed, the air buzzing with celebration. Snow is falling, catching the glow of the streetlights and the massive banners hanging from every building. Everywhere you look, you see the red flags of the Reich, stretching high above the city, glowing under the searchlights sweeping the sky. And the people—thousands of them—cheering, singing, celebrating. The energy is unlike anything I've ever witnessed. Berlin has never felt so alive.

And at the center of it all, the victory parade is moving through the capital. You can hear the thunder of boots on stone— thousands of Wehrmacht soldiers marching in perfect step, row after row, their uniforms crisp, their movements precise. Behind them, the tanks roll forward, their steel hulls shining in the torchlight. Artillery pieces follow, along with captured Soviet banners, trophies of the campaign that brought us here. Every step they take is met with a roar from the crowd, a city full of people showing their gratitude, their pride.

And above us—listen to that! The Luftwaffe is making its presence known. Fighter planes are cutting through the night sky in flawless formation, their engines roaring. The bombers are flying low enough that you can see the markings on their fuselages. Smoke trails and flares streak through the air, painting the sky with light. Children are pointing, their faces full of wonder. I don't think they'll ever forget this moment. I don't think any of us will.

Up on the platform, overseeing it all, are the men who led us to victory. Field Marshals von Bock, von Leeb, and von Rundstedt. They stand still, watching, their expressions unreadable, but you can tell—they know what they've done. They know they've accomplished something no army in history has ever done. And the crowd knows it too. Their names are being chanted through the streets.

And then there's the sound of the church bells ringing in the distance. The hymns from the cathedrals blend with the cheers in the streets. It's Christmas Eve, after all. A fitting night for a victory like this. Some are here for the holiday, some for the Reich, and some for both. But no matter why they're here, they all know one thing for certain.

The war is over. Germany has won.

This is Radio Berlin, signing off from a night we will never forget.

EPILOGUE: Expanding Divergence

I. Consequences of a Different Path

The war in the East brought unimaginable destruction, suffering, and loss. In real history, it dragged on for four years, consuming more than 30 million lives. Entire cities were wiped from existence. The Red Army, battered but relentless, turned the tide in 1943 and marched into Berlin by 1945.

But that history never happened here.

There was no Battle of Stalingrad. No long war of attrition to drain Germany's strength.

There was no Soviet counteroffensive. No Red Army rolling westward to raise its flag over the Reichstag.

There was no divided Europe. No Iron Curtain.

By the end of 1941, the war was over.

The world now faced a German-dominated Europe—an empire stretching from France to the Pacific.

II. Major Reasons for the Different Outcome

The failure of Operation Barbarossa in real history wasn't because of just one mistake. It was a mix of bad strategy, logistical nightmares, and Hitler making the wrong calls at the worst times. But in this version of events, those failures never happened.

Germany didn't have to fight a war in the West. With Britain out of the picture by the end of 1940, the entire Wehrmacht could focus on the Soviet Union. The invasion started a month earlier, giving Germany more time before the brutal Russian winter.

There was no detour to Ukraine. In real history, Hitler split his armies, slowing the push toward Moscow. Here, the Soviet Union fell apart too quickly for that to matter.

The rivalry between German Panzer commanders kept the offensive moving at full speed. The Luftwaffe dominated the skies, crippling Soviet supply lines and wiping out the Red Air Force.

When Moscow fell, so did Stalin. Without him, Soviet leadership collapsed, and the long, grinding war of attrition never happened.

A war that should have dragged on for years ended in months. What should have been Germany's greatest mistake became its greatest victory.

III. Loose Ends & Unanswered Questions

Total victory was achieved. But even as Germany rejoiced, big questions remained.

Siberia was German by treaty, but it hadn't been occupied. No resistance, no government, just vast, frozen emptiness. Would Germany rule it from afar? Would troops be needed?

CASCADING DIVERGENCE 1941 Lebensraum

Or would Hitler take a different approach—one without conquest?

Then there was winter.

The brutal Russian cold had arrived, and the Wehrmacht had to survive it.

Could Germany supply its forces through the long winter?

Would partisans rise up in occupied cities, making consolidation harder?

The Reich had conquered an empire—but now it had to hold it.

And then came the problem of control.

The Red Army was gone, the Soviet Union dissolved—but millions of armed men were still out there.

Disarming Soviet remnants would be Germany's first challenge—ensuring no organized resistance could form.

How would the Reich govern its new empire? Would it rule directly or set up puppet states?

Would Germany's allies—Italy, Japan, and later Finland, which, while not formally an Axis member, was aligned with Germany in the Continuation War—demand their share of the spoils?

While Germany celebrated, the world watched.

Britain remained neutral but wary, its empire intact but its future uncertain.

The U.S., still uninvolved, debated its next move. Would Roosevelt accept this new world order, or was this just the beginning of a bigger confrontation?

Japan saw opportunity. With the USSR gone, was Hitler's Reich an obstacle—or a potential economic partner?

For now, Hitler's empire stretched from Europe deep into the East. The Reich stood at the height of its power.

CASCADING DIVERGENCE 1941 Lebensraum

The Alternate History Continues

Thank you for reading this second novel in the CASCADING DIVERGENCE saga. The world you've entered — reshaped by Churchill's death and the collapse of Britain's resistance — continues to evolve. Each new story in the series builds upon the foundation laid in 1940.

While the main title remains CASCADING DIVERGENCE, each book has a unique subtitle. The subtitles (in bold) and major themes (in parentheses) of the other books in the saga are:

- **1940** (An Alternate World History Begins)
- **1941 Presa d'Africa** (Italy's quest for an African empire)
- **1942 Chūgoku-sen** (Imperial Japan's war in China)
- **1943 Purification** (A holocaust on an unmatched scale)
- **1943 Wunderwaffen** (A superweapons arms race)
- **1944 Coalescence** (A federation of freedom forms)
- **1945 Project Aegis** (The ultimate defensive weapon)

Check the same location where you purchased this book for the availability of other titles in the series.

To be notified of future releases, receive special offers, or share your thoughts on the CASCADING DIVERGENCE universe, please email:

captain.kodos@gmail.com

About the Author

Ron Wood has long been fascinated by the historical complexity and profound human drama of World War II, viewing it as a pivotal conflict between forces of liberty and oppression. His deep interest arises from the awareness of how closely the world once teetered on the brink of a dramatically different future.

An avid visitor to World War II museums and historical landmarks, Ron particularly values personal testimonies from those who lived through the era. His extensive knowledge provides authentic and compelling insights that vividly recreate the tension and high stakes of the time.

Ron's professional career spans engineering, science, invention, strategic business planning, and persuasive communication. His experiences include contributions in aerospace, aviation, cosmology, and technology sectors.

CASCADING DIVERGENCE 1941 Lebensraum

Favoring concise, fast-paced narratives inspired by cinematic storytelling, Ron's writing style is swift and immersive, appealing strongly to readers who prefer gripping, momentum-driven tales over heavily detailed descriptions.

Acknowledgments

While storytelling often unfolds in quiet solitude, the journey from draft to finished book is enriched immeasurably by collaboration with talented and dedicated professionals.

Special thanks to the graphic artist Tabitha Fischer for bringing the setting vividly to life through her beautifully rendered imagery. I also extend my appreciation to my editor, Mary Jean Jones, whose perceptive feedback and unwavering attention to nuance continue to enhance and refine my work. Lastly, my gratitude to the skilled team at Getcovers.com for creating another compelling cover that captures the essence of this story.

Your collective expertise, artistry, and commitment have once again brought my vision vividly into being. Thank you all for your exceptional contributions.

Made in the USA
Monee, IL
03 June 2025